ACCLAIM F

AIREL

"Move over, Twilight. Here comes Aaron Patterson."

—Joshua Graham, bestselling
author of Beyond Justice and Darkroom

"I was surprised by how much I really, really liked this book. I have not jumped on the whole 'fallen angel' bandwagon, just as I didn't jump on all of the vampire stories that came out after Twilight. This is not your typical fallen angel story. It is one that has left me breathlessly waiting for the next one in the series. Hurry up, please..."

—Sandra Stiles

"It takes rare talent for a man to write a novel from a male POV and have it published to great critical and commercial acclaim. But it takes a miracle for that same male—or in this case, males—to write a novel from the POV of a teenage girl and have it turn out as incredibly as did the new StoneHouse YA by Aaron Patterson and Chris White, Airel. From the first sentence, I felt compelled to dive into this young woman's story, and just as importantly, I felt like I personally knew her, which means I laughed, stressed and cried right along with her. A beautifully written and crafted fiction about teenage innocence, faith, loss, and love. A must-read for teens and adults alike."

—Vincent Zandri, International Bestselling
Author of The Remains, The Innocent, and Concrete Pearl.

"An amazing story that will captivate audiences ranging from young adult to the young at heart. Airel crosses boundaries in a fascinating and unforgettable way to engage readers within a story that will not soon be forgotten."

—Amazon Reviewer

"I am happy to say that this novel is one of my favorites of its kind. I never thought I could read a novel like this and be so swept away. I am always willing to try new books, but I usually steer clear of this kind of novel. Not anymore. Not when I can be so engrossed into the character's story, like I was with the beautiful Airel, that before I know, it's over. I kept turning the pages, wanting to—no, NEEDING to know—what was going to happen next."

—Molly Edwards, Willow Spring, NC

"The word 'enjoyed' somehow doesn't express how much, in a positive light, what this book, The Airel Saga, Book 1, gave me. I loved the book and can hardly wait for the sequel. Though the story line is about Airel's teenage experience, I, at 75, truly enjoyed the read and was able to identify with her. As it happened to Airel, I felt it was happening to me."

—*Amazon Reviewer*

ACCLAIM FOR CHRIS WHITE

THE MARSBURG DIARY

"Yikes. This is one well-written and very strange book which will pique your interest from beginning to end. The author does a masterful job of moving you between centuries as you read two different point-of-view stories about one very unusual book. The telling of the tale, as found in the father's diary from the 1800s, is very well portrayed and the writer has you believing you are actually back in that time period. Stepping forward to today, you experience the son's horror as he reads both his father's diary and the unusual book, and discovers it is currently driving him into the same mindset it created in his father—near insanity. This is one roller coaster of a read and is sure to delight fans of the occult, supernatural occurrences, and mystery. A solid 4 1/2 star read."

—*POIA, top Amazon reviewer*

"A story that conjures mystery, suspense, and dark evils, The Marsburg Diary, is a page turner. White calls on the spirits of Steven King, Jules Verne, and Edgar Allen Poe to create a contemporary story that is as compelling as it is enduring. Marsburg learns of his father's past through a diary, a past filled with horror and mystery. But history doesn't stay in the past, and visits Marsburg, sending him into his own thrilling adventures. The Marsburg Diary is to Airel what Torchwood is to Doctor Who—a grownup, stay- up- late, dark theme on a masterful series."

—*Peter Leavell, Meridian, ID*

"I really love Chris White's writing. He's extremely talented and he is quickly becoming a favorite of mine."

—*Michelle Vasquez, Life in Review*

K: [PHANTASMAGORIA]

"Chris White has the talent of long-ago writers interlaced with his own unique voice. Anything this man writes keeps me up. I literally have to schedule time to read his work because I know when I start, I'll not eat, sleep, or bathe until I've finished it. K: [PHANTASMAGORIA] is nothing short of his signature work. In fact, this might be his best novel to date. K is a character that you can't even begin to summarize. His experiences are all too familiar on so many levels. His relationship with others and God is eerily too close to home for not only myself, but so many I know. You simply have to read this book."

—Bri Clark, Meridian, ID

URIEL

The Inheritance

Part Nine
Book 5 in the Airel saga

Aaron Patterson

Chris White

StoneHouse Ink 2014
StoneHouse Ink
Boise, ID 83713
http://www.stonehouseink.net

First eBook Edition: 2014
First Paperback Edition 2014

ISBN: 978-1-938426506

The characters and events portrayed in this book are fictitious. Any similarity to a real person, living or dead, is coincidental and not intended by the author.

Uriel: a novel/by Aaron Patterson & Chris White
Cover design by © Claudia McKinney - phatpuppyart.com
Layout design by Ross burck - rossburck@gmail.com

This book was professionally edited by Tristi Pinkston - http://www. tristipinkstonediting.blogspot.com

Published in the United States of America

StoneHouse Ink

Also by Aaron Patterson

Sweet Dreams (Book 1)
Dream On (Book 2)
In Your Dreams (Book 3)
Breaking Steele
Twisting Steele
Melting Steele
Airel (Book 1)
Airel (Book 2)
Michael (Book 3)
Michael (Book 4)
Uriel (Book 5)
Uriel (Book 6)
19 (Digital Short)
The Craigslist Killer (Digital Short)
Zombie High (Digital Short)
Elena's Secret: A Vampire Diaries story

Also by Chris White

Airel (Book 1)
Airel (Book 2)
Michael (Book 3)
Michael (Book 4)
Uriel (Book 5)
Uriel (Book 6)
The Marsburg Diary (Book 1, Airel Saga novellas)
The Wagner Diary (Book 2, Airel Saga novellas)
The Falkenhayn Diary (Book 3, Airel Saga novellas)
The Great Jammy Adventure of the Flying Cowboy (a children's book)
Strongbox (a digital short)
Amethyst (a digital short)

PART NINE
THE INHERITANCE

CHAPTER I

Cape Town, South Africa—Present Day

"DAD," WAS ALL SHE said.

Kreios fell to his knees in the dirt beside his daughter. His eyes were tender and his voice shook. "Eriel."

She smiled, weak. "Dad, I've told you a thousand times. It's Uriel." She coughed up blood. "I've missed you."

Kreios broke into deep, heavy sobs, weeping bitterly. Thousands of years had passed since she had disappeared. He'd believed she was dead. And now, just when he'd found her again . . . After a few moments he regained his self-control and asked, "What happened?"

"I took the Mark upon myself."

Kreios was stunned and confused. "But why?" was all he could manage. He crouched back on his knees and squeezed his eyes shut, realization sinking in.

"Michael and Airel are…" Uriel began, "…more important."

He looked at her, overcome with sadness. "But you are important to me. I cannot allow this." What then came to him to do was dangerous. But were there any other options?

He closed his eyes and weighed his decision.

Finally he broke the silence. "Airel," he said, his eyes still closed, "Airel, take Michael and your father and get off this mountain."

"What?" she said.

He turned to her and said gently, "It will not be safe for you here. Not for anyone. You must go."

He turned back to his daughter, to his Uriel—his Eriel. More tears escaped from his eyes. "If we . . . if what I am about to do makes an end of my daughter, you must go and find what is next for you. I may not be able to continue on." His tone was flat, resigned. He knew what he was about to do. There was only one choice remaining; there was no sense delaying anything.

He turned and looked straight at Airel. "You are ready; this is what you were born to do. Listen for El and keep your head. Now go."

He turned back to Uriel's sick and dying body. "I must now do what I can for her, and I am afraid. There is not much time left."

"But, Kreios, we—"

"Airel," he thundered, snapping his head to glare at her. Light pulsed from his tattoos; his teeth clenched. "Go now, and do not make me ask again."

Airel turned to go, reluctance written on her every feature.

Uriel looked into her father's eyes with surprise. "No, Father, leave me. Stay with Airel—you must."

But Kreios shook his head and began to open himself to what might very well kill him. This was his daughter, and he would not let her die.

NOT ON YOUR LIFE. No—just try to make me leave you, Kreios.

I wanted to scream at him, but I was confused and still trying to process that Ellie was in fact his daughter. Not only that, but she had saved Michael. At what cost?

"Go," Kreios said again, but this time it was almost a whisper.

My movements felt robotic as I obeyed Kreios. Having only just been reunited with him, I hated the idea of leaving his side again, but he was not taking no for an answer—and I feared what I saw there in his eyes. I turned to see Ellie one last time, the little baby I'd read so much about, the one Kreios lived for, his only daughter. She gripped his shoulder and tried to pull herself up, but she couldn't.

Is this the last time I'll see her? I couldn't speak.

Michael scooped up my father in his arms and carried him. *My mixed-up life will be the death of everyone I love.* I looked on at the limp motionlessness of my dad and wondered if he was going to make it. *Will he live? What has he been through for me? Am I worth all this?*

I looked back at Kreios. I had to fight to hold back tears. He was draped over his daughter's dying body, the muscles of his back jerking in spasms of grief as he sobbed. I wanted to run to him, to help somehow, but I knew—I could feel—this was something far beyond me.

Michael touched my arm and I searched his eyes for some hidden strength. He managed a small smile and said, "Come on, Airel. Let's go home."

FRANK WISEMAN WATCHED THE sun beginning to burst upon the predawn sky over False Bay from the verandah of his posh villa in Simon's Town. He hated it—he hated all of it. His harpy of a wife was scratching and clucking like a yard-bound hen again, nagging him into getting a bit of exercise.

"But you'll live longer," she always said. He hated that too. She only wanted him to live longer so she would have someone to nag. If she didn't have that, she wouldn't have a single reason to live, he ventured.

Nevertheless, he was up at sunrise. Why? Because he was hopelessly stranded in the rut of his life. The truth was, if he didn't have her around to make him miserable, he wouldn't have anything. He had come to enjoy fighting with her. But he never let that show. It would ruin the game for both of them.

"Well, Frank, let's get a move on," she said, her voice strident and grating.

"After you, princess." He used her pet name like an insult.

They walked down the steps together to the beach. She was talking again, and he tuned her out. There was some mention of, "… you've got to quit the salt …" and a little more of, "… at your age, you know …" He rolled his eyes and kept up with her.

The sun was about to peek over the mountains across the bay. It would be blinding and she would go on about how magnificent it was and "Oh, Frank, isn't it lovely to be up and out before the dawn so we can see all this," but it would be blinding anyway and all it would mean was another wretched day had come upon him, that there would be heat, sun, misery, and his dear wife, Kimberley, in increasing order of irritation.

He kicked at a stone embedded in the sand, but his foot caught on it and he took a tumble, soaking his nice new pants in the wet sand. "Ow. Dash it all."

"Frank? Oh, dear. Are you all right?"

"I'm fine. Just help me up, will you?"

She reached to help him. "Are you sure? Did you break

anything? You should be more careful. You know how brittle your bones are."

"No, Kimberley, no broken anything. Lucky for you." He tried his best to dust the sand from his bottom, but he was still wet and uncomfortable. Yes, it was rather like Kimberley.

He looked down at the offending rock, more than a little bemused at the effect it had taken on his morning exercise.

But it was not a rock.

It was something bright pink.

"Well, now, what is that, do you suppose?" he muttered to himself. "Princess, will you help me with this?" He kneeled in the sand to dig around the edges of the object.

The more his hands scraped away the wet sand, the more intrigued he became. He did not know where the impulse was coming from, but it seemed … it seemed … it seemed like something important.

Frank dug while Kimberley stood with her arms crossed, clicking her tongue in disgust.

Finally, the earth gave up its buried treasure. It had been embedded in the sand by the tides. "Some child's book bag," Frank exclaimed, beginning to fumble for the zipper.

"Well, don't open it." she scolded, but he did anyway. "Really. I don't see how it's any of your business, Frank. I really—"

"Kimberley," Frank said in annoyance, "shut up."

She did, but not without a huff and a foot stomp.

The zipper fell back to reveal a bright red jewel. As the sun threw open the day, the first rays fell upon the stone and lit it with an unreal light.

But hold, Frank thought, quite unlike himself, *what's this?* The stone was the most beautiful thing he had ever seen. Still, he wondered what else might be in the knapsack. Perhaps more treasures?

He opened the bag further and looked inside it. "It's a book," he said absentmindedly. "A right nice-looking one, too." He reached to pull it out, and as he did so, his fingers brushed against its hidebound cover. Like a shot in the dark, one word rang out in his head:

AIREL.

CHAPTER II

Arabia—1232 B.C.

URIEL WATCHED FROM THE limbs of a tree high above as her father roared at the heavens in frustration. There was pain there, too. She bore witness to the undeniable fact that this pain was the final thing they now shared. She decided in that moment that it would be the last time they shared anything.

How can I explain myself to a man who refuses to listen, who refuses to allow me to be who I am and not what he wants me to be?

She thought back to all the misunderstandings, all her attempts at flight, thwarted by her father. Each time she tried to spread her wings, he was there to stop her. All he ever did was hold her back, and all in the name of keeping her safe.

I am not a child anymore. Quit treating me like I am made of glass.

She held her breath and closed her eyes, focusing on the thing she wanted most—to disappear, to leave. She knew enough of the shadowing gift to know how to draw the mists about her, as her uncle Yamanu had taught. In this, she had proven to be naturally gifted and able, and it had not occurred to her then that

the expression on Yamanu's face could have been either shocked
surprise or veiled fear when she had done it so easily the first time.
She felt that the gift was different for her than it was for Uncle Yam,
and his eyes had confirmed as much to her mind.

She was able, not just simply to call up a powerful spiritual
fog, but to physically dissemble, the minutest particles of her body
disbanding into the atmosphere. They were bound only by the
invisible, her spirit, which, when she focused hard, commanded
that the air into which she had dissolved would release the infinite
specks that composed her. Then she would resume her natural form.
She had scared herself a few times testing this new power, but in the
end she reasoned, eagles must either fly or die. *If an eagle cannot or
will not fly, it really isn't much of an eagle, is it?*

He would see soon enough that it was not she who needed
protecting.

YAMANU WAS SEIZED WITH terror, which was not like him.
He was customarily the one rational mind, the one trusting and
dauntless spirit composing this angelic fellowship. But now his
thoughts ran wild.

He decided he had to write to Kreios, tell him what he believed
was true, and hope that perhaps he would be able to reach Uriel
before it was too late.

Salutations, Kreios,

*My kinsman and my friend, I fear this letter may reach
you far too late, but I must tell you what I have witnessed
here.*

*Your daughter came to live with me, as you are no doubt
aware. She was a delight, but like you, she has her own mind.*

I sensed a change upon her arrival in Ke'elei. She had travelled so far, and I feared she had been compromised.

As you know, I believe neither in chance nor coincidence.

My kinsman, she arrived at the city already in a state of metamorphosis, though it didn't manifest in sickness until later.

She fell ill for a time. She took on new appetites and her hair changed from raven black to a lighter hue. The first day I noticed it, it took on a purplish cast, and from then on, it became bluer and bluer until she could hide it no longer and went about the city at all times with a scarf covering her head.

The Brotherhood possesses untold power and I began to suspect her change was instigated by a young man she was fond of—a boy named Subedei.

I prayed and asked El to confirm to my heart if she had been activated by the Brotherhood, but I did not receive an answer. I prayed again, but still, only silence.

She begged me to train her in the angelic arts and I, like a fool, began to teach her. To my surprise and dismay, her gift revealed itself as precisely that selfsame shadowcraft I have long possessed. I taught her one lesson. She soon surpassed me in both power and potency.

And now she has taken that immense untested burden and fled. I searched in vain, but she is like the wind. I ask for your mercy and forgiveness in this matter, as I have failed you. I shall live eternally with my regret if anything terrible should befall her.

Your humble kinsman and friend,
Yam

ALL KREIOS COULD DO was nothing, and it threatened to be his undoing. He wanted to fly over the earth and search his daughter out, rip the mountains apart by their roots and turn them to dust.

But he knew his kin was right—she would not be found until she desired such a thing.

He felt sure that he bore the lion's share of the blame for his daughter's waywardness. He had tyrannized her. He hadn't given her enough choices. It was inevitable that she would rebel—he had pushed her away.

Kreios moaned in agony, falling to his knees and touching his brow to the earth, his hands covering his ears in a vain attempt to blot out the sound of his own condemnation. His heart and conscience told him again and again that this turn of events had been of his making. He had backed Eriel into a cage, and in response, she had shaken what she could shake.

And now, as a Shadower, what would she do? Where would she go? This, the most powerful of the angelic arts, had been unlocked in her, and it was like touching a single burning ember to a field of dry stubble. *What will she do with this knowledge, this power, completely unchecked by wisdom, without a mentor or teacher?* The thought was too terrible to bear. Kreios knew his daughter would, as sure as the sun now sank below the horizon in the west, inevitably burn, that it would produce only more pain in her life.

He did not know how to pray. Should he ask for mercy or for punishment? She was out there on her own now. The thought made him groan in deep frustration.

He could no longer protect his own daughter. His one remaining passion and promise—failed.

CHAPTER III

Cape Town, South Africa—Present Day

KREIOS TRIED TO CLEAR his mind, but thoughts of past failures and losses plagued him. Uriel, his only daughter, was not dead but alive, and here. He wanted to ask her why. He wanted to curse her for leaving him, for allowing him to think she was dead. He was torn between his role as a father and his love for her. Duty or unconditional love? One would think that the choice would not be so hard.

But she now lay dying. "Uriel, you must not move. No matter what happens now, do not try to intervene."

Her eyes stayed half open and unfocused as a long, miserable moan escaped her parted lips. She was on the edge of consciousness; her skin was clammy white, and the stench from the Mark was strong.

Kreios closed his eyes and opened his mind to the heavens, to El, beholding his daughter with new eyes. Veins of black ran over the skin of her arms and neck, twisting, choking vines of death.

He placed his hand over her heart. "El ..." Kreios, the Angel of Death, whispered a prayer. In his mind he could see the door, dark and broken as if somewhere in time, it had been burned. Red light seeped from the corners and between the broken slats of wood. Beyond was the Mark, his curse, and maybe his very life.

Kreios reached for the door and flung it open.

ELLIE SAW THE EARTH open beneath her, beheld Sheol opening its gaping jaws to receive her, and though she closed her eyes to blot out the sight of it, the vision wouldn't respond. Her mind still stared on. A great cord, a black vine had grown out from the darkest recesses of the earth, its roots suckling on the surges of a blood-red stone, the vine opening its hideous tendrils to receive her, and as these wisps of blackness wended themselves around her body and constricted her, she held fast to her final strand of hope—that all was not lost.

Then a bolt of light shot past her from above and behind, smote the hideous vine with a powerful blow, and she was free. She turned to the sky—light.

Below—darkness.

Blood.

Kreios.

Breaking from the vision, her eyes flew open and she gasped for air, clutching at her chest. She coughed and spit up a dark slime that sizzled when it hit the dirt. She was alive and at once remembered where she was, who had saved her, and what that could mean.

She sat up, feeling her strength return to her in powerful waves. She looked around for Kreios, fearing the worst. "Father?"

But she was alone.

FRANK WISEMAN WASTED NO time. "Come here, princess," he said to Kimberley, "and help me up, dear." As his wife came near and grasped his hand, he stared into her eyes. *She feels enough to fear. But not enough to know what I'm going to do to her.*

Frank stood to his feet, but did not let go of her hand. He wheeled her around, jamming her hand into the small of her back as he marched her into the dawn surf, deeper. Deeper.

"What are you up to now? You fancy a swim? But you hate the water—Frank, stop messing around and let me go."

Kimberley made an attempt to break free. But Frank pushed on as the water came up chest-high. He felt her body tense up as what he was about to do started settling in. He wondered if she would fight it, lie to herself so her own reality would override her fears.

Frank leaned into her ear as the surf rose and whispered, "Shh." When the next wave came, he grabbed the back of her head and forced her under. *A person can drown in a couple of centimeters of water.* She struggled but he held her fast, not letting up.

When the wave had passed them by and she tried to cough it out, he covered her nose and mouth with his free hand. *Instinct. She's a good girl—she wouldn't struggle on purpose.*

Another wave, and as she fought harder, he held her under, letting his head fall back, allowing the red sun to bathe his face in its warmth. This was the moment, the most sublime feeling he had ever experienced. How could taking a life feel so … so right?

Frank could feel the undertow working on his body from about the knees down. He pushed with one hand and pulled her hair with the other, getting his knee wedged into her back. He was amazed at his own strength; he wondered at how young he felt. Getting rid of the baggage was doing him wonders.

The thrashing stopped. When he felt the fingers of the undertow grasping for Kimberley's body, he released her and she slipped away from him forever. *Perhaps she'll stay down under a thermocline for a while. Until the sharks get her.*

Perhaps one already had. He waded back to the shore, and as he did, a sense of relief filled him.

The pink backpack was still there on the beach. He snatched it up and walked casually to the house, where he took off his wet clothes and then, naked, held the stone up to the sunlight. It whispered something he couldn't put into words; it was more of a feeling than a tangible voice.

"You know where I should go," Frank said absently, "and I know who to call." He set the stone—the Bloodstone, he thought he should call it, and chuckled at his originality—up on a makeshift shrine near the window, where it could catch the sun's rays.

The room became red. Frank giggled like he hadn't done since he was in primary school. He dialed the number and waited for someone to pick up on the other end.

CHAPTER IV

Boise, Idaho—Present Day

MICHAEL HAD NEVER HAD as many questions in his life as
he did now. And yet the power of his love for Airel compelled him
to place them all aside as he looked on and saw her mourning in
the rain at Kim's open grave. Already, she looked older and more
mature.

He understood grief. He also understood what it felt like to
bear too much—experience. Whether such things would produce
wisdom, or indeed, anything good, remained to be seen. What he
did know was that he wouldn't say much today. What was there to
say at the mouth of a grave?

The plane ride back from Africa had been surreal. Airel's father,
John, was stoic. *Stoic doesn't even begin to describe him.* After the
fog of whatever sedative he had been dosed with finally burned off,
he'd hardly spoken to Michael the whole trip home. All he had said
was, "You can call me Mr. Cross." And that was what plenty of
people called him on the way home, all of them showing the most
profound respect.

John Cross seemed to blame Michael for everything. Each

sideways glance said more than any words ever could. *He blames me.*

Michael wasn't entirely certain how they had been allowed to pass through customs—if that was what two armed guards, a private hangar, and a chartered jet amounted to—but he did hear *diplomat* bandied about more than once in hushed tones, along with the word *president,* but exactly which president, and of what country, he didn't know. The expressions of awe and fear on the faces of those who attended them, the fact that eye contact was always deferred, said more. Michael wondered what kind of pull John Cross had with the authorities. It was internationally potent, whatever it was, and they clearly were going to be allowed to leave South Africa and enter the United States without documentation of any kind, absolutely incognito. His mind spun with a million questions, but the look John had given him … that stopped everything.

So they had spent the next twenty-four hours travelling on a chartered plane. It was a small aircraft and didn't have provision for baggage beneath, so Kim's coffin—an unceremonious-looking air freight crate—rode with them in the back of the passenger cabin all the way back to Boise. A load-keeping curtain had been strapped down between the "cargo" and their seats, but still.

They had touched down in Boise yesterday and nothing really happened after that, except for this—sometime in the early evening, John walked up to Michael, shook his hand firmly, and looked him in the eye. He said, "Thank you. Thank you for all you've done for my daughter. I'm very sorry for *your* loss." Michael understood that John was talking about Stanley. He figured Airel must have had a sit-down with John and asked him to go easy on him, telling him he had nowhere to go, nowhere to live, nowhere even to sleep, but all he had been able to do was nod.

And now today, at Kim's grave, he couldn't even do that.

He stood wordlessly outside the inner circle and watched Airel grieve the loss of her best friend. *If anyone in this whole mess was innocent, it was Kim.*

At least at first.

ELLIE STOOD IN THE rain under a leafless tree wearing gray skinny jeans and a black zippered hoodie, the hem of the hood brought down low over her forehead. She looked on at the mourners. There was something like pity in her eyes as they beheld the sight of the girl's mother—a divorcée and single mother who, Uriel knew enough from her due diligence on Airel, had tried her best for Kim. But now the time in yet another human life had run its course, and those who were left had to find a way to move on.

Unfortunate that Kim got caught up in this. Uriel reflected on her own past, on her own dealings with the Brotherhood, on what she had learned over the course of millennia. Kim had been smart enough to do reasonably well in life, at least before it had gained an infinite number of extra dimensions. The Bloodstone had simply been overwhelming to her, in every possible way. *And in some impossible ways.*

Ellie looked at Airel and rubbed at her chest where the Mark had gripped her. Airel was so similar to how she had been at that age. She was one whose mind was usually made up without the benefit of very many unbiased facts. Ellie sighed. *What am I going to do about you, Airel?*

It was indeed time to move on. She turned and walked away in the rain. She felt like herself once again, no longer Uriel—the name of her youth—but Ellie. Echoes of her father calling her name, usually the wrong one, resounded in her head. She would, she decided, let the old names die with the old memories. *Is there any other choice?*

She needed time to grieve, time to think. And she knew where she could go.

Home.

I COULDN'T MAKE MYSELF become fully present at Kim's grave. My mind was elsewhere. Random thoughts kept pressing into me even as I watched the casket hang above the open hole on wide canvas straps in the pelting rain.

She? I couldn't tell if it was me or her anymore sometimes, but the phrase, *"The Shining Ones"* kept skittering into and out of my head, along with something that sounded Arabic, something that sounded like *Derakhshan,* but it was slightly different.

I sighed and shivered. Though my mom held an umbrella over me, I almost didn't want it. I wanted to feel the cold rain drenching me. *Maybe that would wake me from this trance. I feel like nothing's real anymore.*

"God, Kimmie. I am going to miss you." I started to cry again, and fear rose up and seized me once more. It was so real, so final, so rude and sudden and scary that Kim could *die.* That she *could* die. And if she could, that meant I could, that anyone I loved could as well, and that this pain I now felt would never find an end, never resolve into healing.

Is this my life? To outlive everyone I love, to endure and go on as if my old human life was a whisper?

I scooped some of the moist earth up into my hands and placed it on top of Kim's casket. Michael held me, and I was so glad he was with me. He didn't say anything. But he was there. I didn't know if I could go on without him; he was the man I wanted to be with. There was no other for me.

Heat filled my eyes and the tears spilled over, uncontrolled. This was all on me—Kim's death, the reason she was even there in that stupid wooden box was all on me.

I didn't want any of this. Somewhere deep inside me, hidden between the folds of my heart, I knew I was meant for something. I didn't know what it was Yet.

THAT NIGHT, I SAT on the couch with my family at home, staring into space, the TV newscast running over me. I, like a boulder in a swift torrent, sat unmoved. My mind hovered over my best friend's grave. I was in shock.

I couldn't believe that Kim, my Kimmie, was gone, that her life was over. She hadn't even turned eighteen yet. Then again, neither had I. I couldn't help thinking that when I did turn another year older, and it was inevitable, that I would be forced to move on without her, and for every year after that for the rest of my life. We would not see each other anymore. There would be no more breakfasts at Sunrise Café, no more movie nights and long talks.

That event—the date that would mark what would have been Kim's next birthday—was months away, and I had to admit to myself that the "moving on" part was never going to happen for me. I would never forget Kim, never let her go or let myself stop hurting. But she had been doomed before Africa. Before Ascension Island and Wideawake Airfield. Before we left the House of Kreios in our ambitious quest to—*to do what? Save the world? Change the world?*

The newscast was an incoming tide—*Authorities aren't giving*

*any details, but sources say a local girl has returned home from
a frightening abduction that took her all the way to Africa. Our
investigative journalist, Les Wright, has more on this possible
human trafficking ring*— and it rose and fell over me like waves—
*and join me on location in Eagle. Sources also say that there were
two minors involved, possibly three, one of them a boy named
Michael Alexander, who had just moved into the area. This might
provide the link to the mysterious disappearance of Eagle resident
Stanley Alexander, the boy's father. It's their house you see behind
me here. Mr. Alexander, Stanley Alexander, has now been missing
for nearly two weeks and is presumed to be*—and all I could do was
breathe in stutters from having wept my eyes out.

Whatever I was going to do, I didn't want to hide. I didn't want
to run from the facts. I didn't want to try to act like everything
would be okay, because it wouldn't be. I knew I would never be the
same.

"I'm going nuts," I said, and I meant it.

"You are nuts," Michael said. "We all saw it a long time ago,
but telling a crazy chick she's crazy is … well … crazy." He was
the only one laughing at his joke, and I could imagine the death
glare my dad was giving him. Michael was sitting on the couch
behind me and I sat between his legs on the floor. He ran his fingers
through my hair, and somehow it made me feel better. I was glad
Michael was not treating me with kid gloves, like my parents. He
made me feel normal, like things might turn out okay. I told him, "I
must be crazy. I like you."

"Sanest thing you ever did."

My dad cleared his throat and I almost giggled, but all that
came out was a coughing choke. "How about pizza?" Dad said. "I'll
buy."

"I could eat," Michael said, jumping up and taking half my hair with him.

"Hey, easy with the hair." I managed to hit him in the back of the leg before he could dodge me.

"Flying Pie or nothing though, okay?" Dad said.

"Sure," Michael said. "Have you seen my cell phone, Airel?"

I shook my head and he walked to the kitchen. I endured the trial that was my new life—parents. So good at times, so lame at others.

"Found it," Michael called out from the kitchen.

"Airel, honey," my mom said, moving behind me now that Michael had stood up, "are you going to be all right? She began to rub my shoulders.

I sighed. "Kim's gone, Mom."

She didn't say anything. Maybe she *couldn't* say anything.

I was both glad to be home—around my parents—and totally claustrophobic about it. I knew they had done their best for me, but somehow I didn't belong here. I felt like a stranger in my own home.

I lived my life believing the whole time that I was invincible, that it would never end. And then one day, poof—time's up. I breathed raggedly, my lungs still spastic from sobbing.

Across the room, my dad stared at the television in a trance. I'd had a heart-to-heart with my parents when we got home from Africa and my dad informed me that I was "not to see Michael anymore." I countered that I was in love with Michael, but Dad shut down and checked out like he always did.

"We love you, honey," my mom said, snapping me out of it. "Know that your father and I are here if you need to talk."

I nodded, but closed my eyes. They were dry; they stung when I blinked, so I kept them closed.

Michael walked back into the room and said, "I tried to get

one with rhinoceros, but they said they were clean out. Went with pepperoni and extra cheese instead."

I turned to face him. He stood over me with a big dumb smile and I pulled him down next to me. I was glad for one thing—Michael *got* me. He understood me. It was such a stupid thing, too, but cracking a joke at the most inappropriate moment was the Kimmiest thing to do, and it was what she would have wanted. The last true thing we ever did together was wrestle on the grass in that park in Arlington, where she swore she was hungry enough to eat a dead rhinoceros. I looked at my mom, who seemed a little concerned about this whole rhinoceros thing. "Don't worry, Mom." I patted her hand. "Inside joke."

I would miss Kim fiercely.

And … I knew this to my core … one day I would avenge her death.

Chapter V

IT WAS LIKE MY life had been wrenched into reverse. I sat on the couch with Michael while my mom sat across from us in her chair, acting nervous with her hands on her thighs, and my dad stalked the living room floor like an inquisitor. What, I thought, are we suddenly Amish, and we have rules for courting now? After all that's happened, I have to ask your permission to live my own life?

"Airel," my dad said, "after all that's happened, I would like you to please explain to me your side of the story. I need to know what has been happening with you and him." He thrust a finger in Michael's direction.

Before I could say anything, Michael jumped in. "Mr. Cross, my dad was an exporter." He just blurted it right out.

"Michael, don't feel like you have to explain for me," I said.

"No, I want to clear this up. It won't be easy, but I want to do it." He turned toward my father. "He told me himself. Stanley Alexander was an exporter of . . . of slaves, okay? He was a human trafficker. He sold people, mostly young girls, and it was probably an international thing." He paused for a moment, taking his time. "As I think back on it—and I've been doing a lot of thinking lately—it seems like it would make sense that he'd been doing it for years. I never dreamed he was—I didn't think that kind of thing could even happen, much less that my own father would ever be involved in something so evil. But I have to face the facts.

"I thought he was a lawyer. I guess he probably did know at least a little bit of law. But the way he put it into practice was criminal. People are supposed to study law to protect the innocent and uphold justice. Not take it apart and abuse it." He exhaled. "I never bothered to ask, because as a kid, you trust your parents, but … I guess that explains why we moved around so much."

There was silence. Michael continued. "I learned how to make friends pretty fast and easy. Every time we moved again, the routine got easier." He ran a hand through the soft spikes of his hair and growled low, an expression of frustration. "I don't have any evidence for this, but I think it's pretty obvious—Stanley used me to scout for new recruits. I would make friends with new kids everywhere we went, and then he would—I guess—snatch them up and ship them off to the distributor."

"The distributor," my mom said.

My dad placed a hand on my shoulder. "Michael, what in the world are you talking about? This doesn't sync up with the information I was able to gather by reading wire reports and the AP feed."

"The AP feed," Michael said, "isn't the last word on what really goes on out there, and every 'news' outlet has at least a little propaganda in it."

"Okay. You've summed up eleventh-grade civics. Good. And thanks for the reminder. But are you trying to tell me that your father—Stanley—was the bad guy here? What about this stalker guy, this blond-haired giant who happened to show up in all the wrong places? What about him?"

"Dad—" I said, but he interrupted me.

"No, Airel. He's a big boy. Let him answer for himself."

"Dad," I said, "you're being unnecessarily harsh, don't you think? Michael has—I mean, he lost his dad."

My dad sighed. "I'm sorry. I'm sorry. But I would still like an explanation. I chased you guys halfway across the world to find you." He fell quiet, and I could imagine that he probably felt a little powerless since, in the end, anyway, he hadn't really done anything except fall into the clutches of a kind of darkness he couldn't have imagined. He'd been drugged, thankfully, so he missed the scariest parts, but then he had reawakened only to see my face, and Michael's too, in that little out-of-the-way hotel room in Simon's Town. Thank God he'd been able to get us home, but still, he had his many questions, and justifiably so. Everything in the middle was still a big blank for him, one that Michael and I would have to fill in very carefully. I took a breath and let it out, hoping Michael had a believable ending and that he would get to it quickly.

"Sir," he said, addressing my dad, "the truth is that Stanley, my father, was the villain in this whole thing. You probably can't imagine how much it hurts for me to be able to admit that, but it's true. I confronted him about it, and he confirmed things that are too crazy for me to make up, the things I told you about his occupation or … hobby.

"What really happened was this—he sent one of his agents to the theater on the night the blond stalker first appeared. This guy— not the blond guy, but the other guy, the one who was killed that night—was a thug. He was supposed to snatch Airel and Kim right then. My—I mean, Stanley–told me everything. The 'blond giant' you're talking about, whoever he is, actually intervened on their behalf."

"What, by murdering this 'thug' guy in public and then

cornering my daughter in the women's room?"

"I don't know what that was all about, truthfully," Michael said. "All I know is that the blond guy got us to safety before Stanley could take Airel." Michael's voice became lower. "But it was too late for Kim."

My dad sighed, and I could tell that he wanted to argue about it. *Come on, Michael, dress this thing up a little better for us.* I couldn't interject without giving the impression that I was helping him make everything up as he went along, and I further knew that *now* wasn't the time to be spilling all the beans about angels and demons. My parents didn't need anything more to freak out about.

"The problem was," Michael continued, "that we didn't know the blond giant was the good guy. See, he was trying to keep us safe, but we resisted him and escaped. Unfortunately, that played right into Stanley's hands."

"Airel, why didn't you just come *home?*" my mom asked, her hand balled up into a fist, tears smearing her eyes. "Wouldn't you have been safe here? Why didn't you let the police handle this?"

I reached out to her. "Because, Mom. I didn't want to put you and Dad in any danger."

"That is so selfish of you, Airel," she cried, and then hid her face behind her hands and collapsed into my dad, who sat down on the arm of her overstuffed chair and held her.

After a while, my dad said calmly, "So what happened in Oregon?"

"Stanley got the upper hand," Michael said. "He and his operatives kidnapped us and flew us to South Africa."

"And then?" My dad was calm and cool; it was alarming.

"We were able to break free from our captors while the deal was being made on the docks in Cape Town. We fled to Simon's Town, where we scraped together enough cash for a room, and we hid there."

"And when or how did I come back into the picture again?" my dad asked.

"There was a knock at the door at about three a.m. We opened it to find you passed out on the floor with your hands and ankles bound. The rest is exactly like we told you that day, sir. We pulled you inside and did our best to try to keep you safe," Michael said. "And then you woke up, made a few phone calls, and we were on our way home."

Our house was so quiet, I could hear the neighbor's radio playing classic rock in his garage with the door down. *Or maybe that's my new super-power-activated angel blood playing up again.* My dad was silent for a long time. My mom had recovered—mostly.

Finally, Dad spoke. "I don't like it. There are too many holes. Michael, are you sure you're telling me everything, son?"

Michael nodded. "Everything I can remember, sir. I was out of it for quite a while too."

Actually, that's true. In fact, most of what Michael had said, though shot through with lies, at least contained somewhat of an element of truth. *I guess he learned these techniques from the Brotherhood. I shouldn't be shocked, or even surprised.*

"What about you, Airel?" my dad asked. "Does this jibe with what you remember?"

Only old people say words like "jibe." "Dad, I was the crazy girl who was so out of it that I thought I'd been gone for months when I finally called you. Remember? When that Agent Reid lady told me that I'd only been missing for like, thirty-six hours? I think I was drugged too, most the time, so everything is all mixed up in my head."

My mom groaned.

"Gretchen Reid," my dad said. "I remember. She's also dead," he said matter-of-factly. "A lot of people are dead. Your blond giant 'good guy' left a trail of it—death and destruction all the way from Portland to Cuba to Cape Town. Unless, of course, there's a mass murderer out there who looks exactly like him. I've done my own research."

"I know, Dad," I said.

"No, you don't know, Airel," my dad said, his voice rising. "The people involved are still out there. What's to stop them from coming after both of you again? You don't know what it's like to nearly lose your only child. And you don't know what kind of people these are."

"Oh, and you do?" I asked. "You do, Dad? How?"

"That's neither here nor there."

"Whatever. Listen, I may not be an adult yet *officially*, but I turn eighteen soon, and you know what? I get to celebrate that birthday without my best friend because *she's* dead too. She doesn't get any more birthdays. And *I* get to go on without her. So don't preach to me for being young and/or ignorant of the evils in the world. I've seen plenty of it, enough to know that you guys," I motioned to both of my parents, "can't keep me safe anymore. I need to make my own decisions."

"Not while you're under my roof," my dad said. "You still have school to finish, and quite a bit of catching up to do. And a lot of learning yet."

He paused. I knew what was coming.

"Airel," he said, "I think it's best if you and Michael take a break from one another until things settle down."

I knew it! "So . . . what, you're going to come to my classes at school and make sure we don't speak there either?" It was just like Dad to circle the wagons and try to establish control in a crisis. And now, just like Michael's story, my whole life was going to have nothing but holes in it. Dad knew how much Michael meant to me now. How much I needed him in order to be able to get through all this pain and loss. Why was he doing this to me?

"Airel, it's for your own good, sweetheart," my mom said, obviously backing her husband's play like a "good wife". That made me so angry, I couldn't see straight. "You'll thank us," she went on, "years from now. You need to finish school—make that your priority."

"Yeah, but how? How can I go back, after all that's happened?"

"After all that's happened," my dad said. "Yes. Your mother and I feel this is what's best for you, Airel."

Chapter VI

WHAT WAS BEST FOR me turned out to be a pretty easy test for me to pass—at least, at first. Two days hadn't gone by before my mom told me she had convinced Dad to allow me to see Michael, but I would have an early curfew now.

"So I need to be home by eight? No exceptions?"

"Not unless you want to be grounded," she said, brushing my hair out of my eyes.

I smirked and sighed in resignation. I felt pulled in five hundred directions at once. I wanted to come back home forever, have it be like it was before I learned I was half angel. But I also felt smothered here, like I was, well, drowning.

Getting back into the routine at school was as daunting to me as preparing for an ascent of Everest. I thought it was going to kill me. I knew I was going to face memories of Kim everywhere and I also thought I would be the class pariah, now not invisible but instead, untouchable.

To my great surprise, though, people were pretty decent and sensitive. My teachers helped me out with all my catch-up work, which, weirdly, only amounted to a couple of weeks of stuff for all the time I felt I'd spent Out There, growing up. And after everyone had gawked at me for a few days, the braver ones actually walked up to me and gave me notes expressing their condolences about Kim. There was real face-to-face relationship stuff happening. Part of that weirded me out a little. But things settled down and I got into a kind of groove. A rhythm.

I still had nightmares. Flashbacks. And I still had a lot of questions, too.

Michael was there, he was always there, and we shared the *Thing Secret* between us about Africa, about all that had been done and all that had precipitated our time there. We would sometimes sit together for lunch and he would ask me, "Do you think they're okay, wherever they are?" and I would know exactly who he was talking about—Kreios and Ellie—and I would give him a kind of noncommittal answer, a ho-hum-I-suppose.

The truth was, I didn't know the first thing about my angelic grandfather or his only daughter. Though it felt cold and harsh, I thought sometimes they might be gone—dead—and this one thought actually helped me to believe that one day, I might be able to move on with my life.

Christmas break started to beckon in the wane of a rough December, and it was much colder than it normally was in Boise. I had settled back into my American teenager life, my student career path, even having made a few new friends. Life felt normal.

And I wanted that.

Most of me, anyway.

Sawtooth Mountains of Idaho—Present Day
HIGH UP IN THE Sawtooth Mountains, Ellie took her time in her

father's house. It was a far cry from where she grew up, but he had both the time and the resources to build it the way he wanted it. The emptiness of the corridors saddened her, though, because without Kreios, this house was an empty building made of stone and metal.

Where are you? She reached out again, standing on the porch that overlooked the meadow below. A young eagle bellowed its flight call, and the peal echoed over the green landscape.

Ellie gave up, frustrated. Kreios was either dead or somehow beyond her reach. She prayed to El that it was the latter.

Something about Airel's father, John Cross, bothered her. He, like his daughter, had a secret. The more she pondered it, the more it unsettled her.

South Africa and the circumstances surrounding their return didn't add up. He knew more than he let on—he *was* more than he let on. Ellie pored over book after book in her father's library, trying to trace her lineage. She looked for the link from Kreios to Airel, but a huge part was missing. John Cross was not mentioned in the line of the Sons of El.

Am I going about this all wrong? Could it be her mother who is in the line?

Ellie ran her hand through her electric blue hair and muttered a string of curses in her native tongue, words that expressed her true feelings. *This is going to be harder than I thought.*

Boise, Idaho—Present Day

I WAS AT SCHOOL walking down the hall to math class a couple of days later when I saw it—blue hair bobbing up and down in a sea of teenagers hurrying to their final class of the day. There was a little pompom of neon coming toward me, converging on the same door I was headed to. We met at the threshold simultaneously, and I couldn't believe my eyes.

"Hey, girlie. Howzit?"

I dropped my textbook and hugged her savagely. "Ellie."

CHAPTER VII

Arabia—1230 B.C.

URIEL HAD BEEN FORCED to meet with Anael well out of the way, in an inconvenient place. The Brotherhood's draining draw had been a significant concern to him, but he didn't know her very well yet, didn't know that she could shadow even the draw and eliminate all trace of her true allegiance with the Brotherhood. It was no matter. Caution was certainly merited at this stage of their uneasy conspiracy.

So she had agreed to meet him well outside the walls of Ke'elei, in the bowels of the forest, in the darkest stage of the night so that the conference between him, the leader of the angelic council at Ke'elei, and Uriel, the living catalyst who would be its undoing, could take place.

Anael, an ancient-looking figure crowned and bearded and robed with white, walked delicately into the clearing where she waited, concealed not by her supernatural talents but by her black cloak, by fronds of fern and tangles of creeping vines on rotting trunks. "Traitor, speak," he said. "Show thyself."

Uriel emerged from the darkness and felt the pale light of a slivered moon illuminating her features. She pulled back the hood of her cloak and allowed the sickly light to fall upon the unnatural hair of her head, like the breast feathers of a tropical bird. Out here, away from all constraint and rule, she could be who she really was. Out here, outcast, she could leave Eriel, her erstwhile friend Santura, and Kreios, Zedkiel—even Uncle Yamanu behind. "I am here."

Anael smiled at her. It was veiled with a sprinkling of fatherly benevolence, making it all the more chill, dread, and evil. "I am glad indeed to see that I have not labored in vain, child."

"Let us be quick about our business," she said. "The forest might house a witness against us if we remain too long here."

Anael agreed with a nod. "You must know, then, what I require as payment for the surrender of the council's plans and strategy?"

"I am able to guess," Uriel said, spitting onto the mossy earth. "Do I need to speak it aloud here, or no?"

"No indeed, for I shall speak it for you. You will bring me the red stone that hangs from the neck of the Seer."

"A different man now holds that office, old one. Kreios punished my master in the clipping of one wing, as well as the slaying of his slave and host. You must know that such a request is … that it would be impossible for anyone but me to fulfill it."

"Yes, I am aware of your talents." He waved his hand in dismissal and disdain. "What I am not yet assured of, though, is the quality of your character—whether I can trust you to follow through on our bargain."

She scoffed and wiped her mouth with the back of her hand. "Can two traitors ever trust one another?" She dissolved from his sight in an instant, reappearing on a limb above and behind him. "A better question, old one," she said, waiting for him to turn toward her, "would be to ask yourself if you *want* to trust me." She dissolved again, reappearing directly in front of him, right in his face, saying, "Or even more, if you can afford *not* to."

Anael smirked at her, unperturbed. "Talents aplenty. If I did what my rash thoughts now suggest to me, I would try to choke the life out of you." He shrugged. "But I know you could easily escape my grasp." He paused, regarding her. "I also know what motivates you." He stepped closer and she took a step back, the closeness unwelcome. He looked down on her and continued. "I know how powerful it is, vengeance. All that pain and suffering. The sure knowledge that what you suffered, and at the hand of your own father, no less, wasn't the product of love, or even of a modicum of fatherly concern. I know what you feel, child—that it was spite. That he hated you for killing his beloved as you entered this world, and now blames you," his eyes widened and intensified, "for everything."

Uriel stepped back once more and raised her hand against him. "Stop. Enough."

"I know," Anael continued, "that what fuels your fire is your father's regret. That he regrets having ever come here to begin with. That he regrets having loved and lost. That he regrets *you,* most of all, and that he sees not a daughter when he looks upon you, girl. I know what he sees."

Uriel gritted her teeth. "Cease."

"He sees in you his eternal punishment."

"Stop." she demanded, and though her intent was to brandish forceful tones, the word exited her lips desperate and petulant.

He relented. "Oh, I can trust you, girl. I know that I can trust you. And your hatred. For such things also fuel my fires."

She pushed him backward. "I care not."

"Liar."

"You can have the bloody stone. I revel in the fall of great kingdoms."

"Fill up your cup with potent revenge, then, for you shall drink your fill, girl, and have all you want of it."

She crossed her arms. "Agreed."

"Our pact is firm." Anael turned back toward Ke'elei.

"When next we meet, we shall together overthrow two dominions."

"Yes," he called to her over his shoulder. "Under the great tree."

She watched him depart the clearing. She then dissolved into the air, invisible, undetected, the perfect infiltratrix.

CHAPTER VIII

Cape Town, South Africa—Present Day

FRANK WAS OVERJOYED; NEW and terrible strength coursed through him. Those who moved past him as he walked through the airport couldn't know how awesome it was, how truly awesome. The power, the elation, the strength, the clean black redness of the whole world ticked along like a well-oiled machine, and he was its master. He was its engineer.

Ticking clocks and Swiss watches, Frank thought. *How keen I now am.* He noticed things he hadn't seen before—puddles of rank water, collections of ruddy dirt in the crevices of long hallways, the shining brown shells of cockroaches crawling, filthy beggars and street children who smelled … sweeter.

But now he approached the gate for his flight to Zurich. It would have irritated him that he had to stop off in Johannesburg and Amsterdam on the way, back when he was somebody else. But now Frank was somebody new. Somebody powerful. Someone who knew how to kill, knew from *personal experience,* and wasn't afraid to do it again.

"Boarding pass, please," the flight attendant said, her palm out, a plastic smile on her face.

Frank produced the document and looked at her chest. The name tag said "Emerald", which shocked and pleased him. "What a brilliant name," he said. "I've never met a girl by the name of Emerald."

She tore off the stub and handed him his pass. "Ja, well, my surname's Ruby, so you can imagine the kind of life I've had to lead, especially in school." She smiled.

Frank decided that the smile wasn't genuine. But he also decided that he liked her in ways that made him feel especially dirty, which suited his new tastes just fine. "Are you flying with us to Schiphol, or only taking tickets?" he asked her.

"Ja, to Amsterdam. And then on to Zurich." She tapped his still-outstretched boarding pass, which showed his connection to Zurich. "Just like you, Mr. Wiseman."

"Ah." *Mr. Wiseman.* Echoes of another life. That made him feel old. And she was less than half his age. "Well, I look forward to seeing more of you," he said.

She smiled again, rocking forward on her toes and then back down. "Well, maybe I can swap with Tanya for the first class cabin."

"I should like that, if you could."

"Only if you promise to tip me well," Emerald said, winking at him as he moved down the jetway. She then greeted the next passenger.

Frank was rather loving this new life. Now that he was finally free of that idiot harpy Kimberley to whom he had been married for all those years, he felt emancipated, new, fresh. Like anything was possible.

Frank stuffed his carryon bag—which contained the rare book—in the compartment above and then settled his corpulent frame into the fragrant leather seat. He could smell the body oils previous occupants had deposited there and that was a pleasing potpourri, a medley of stenches that he wondered how he ever did without now that it was ever present.

What would the stone endow upon him next? He felt himself becoming excited at the prospect, imagining things. He thought of Emerald. He wondered what was going to be on the menu for the in-flight meal. He sniffed. *Some sort of beef dish.* This was a fun new game. Frank fondled the stone in his vest pocket and let his mind go free.

CHAPTER IX

Elsewhere...

KREIOS LAY ON THE cold ground, aware only that he was alive. The dreams he'd had, where he'd gone in order to save his daughter—he could no longer remember these things. All he knew was that El was not finished with him yet, his life was of use, and that he had more to accomplish.

The Mark was gone, ripped from his daughter and also taken from him. He wondered at these things. But he knew El did things as He saw fit and in His own timing. Who was Kreios to question that?

Standing naked, he lifted himself into the air and surveyed his surroundings. He was in the depths of a forest. Where was unclear—it would take some time for him to be able to find his way home again. He had not ascended to heavenly realms. The light of the fallen sun still reflected its rays and warmth off his marble-white body. The only thing he was unsure of was *when* he was. Time could be a funny thing when the thin places of the world were growing, spreading like a virus.

He swelled with power in the sunlight, testing what remained to him since he had taken on the curse of the Mark.

He had his life. That was enough; what more could he ask for?

His tattoos flared brilliant in the light and he lowered himself to the ground, bowing low. He drew on more power than he had ever tasted, and this gift humbled him beyond words.

Some prayers were indeed silent and some things El granted were more than mercy.

El truly was good.

CHAPTER X

Boise, Idaho—Present Day

I MANAGED TO GET inside the door, with Ellie only a step behind, when the bell rang.

"Okay, class, let's get started," Mr. Dorsey, the math teacher, said. "First, we have a couple of new students to introduce." He motioned to a sullen-looking guy in the back of the classroom, an attractive guy with black hair. He dressed like he was in a band; he came off a little emo, yet self-assured. "This is Dirk Elliott. He just moved to Boise from Orange County." Dirk barely looked up in response. I thought he was either really shy or that he was suffering from New Guy Syndrome. *Maybe it's like Invisible Girl Syndrome. I know what that's like.*

Mr. Dorsey then waved a hand at us. "And this, if you ladies will please find a seat, is Ellie Söderström. She moved here all the way from South Africa. All right." He moved quickly into the lesson with no valuable segue of any kind. And I had expected Ellie to wax scandalous about being a bone-white African-American, too.

I was in a lurch. I couldn't believe Ellie was here. And that she was okay. *The one thing I want to do is sit and talk for hours, but I can't do that with her, not here in pre-calc.* I felt like a secret agent who was in danger of blowing her cover if she did anything dumb.

We sat at the two remaining empty desks, and then I turned to her. "So," I said, "how are you, Grandmother?" My tone dripped with sarcasm.

"Shut your face, girlie, or you'll get me in trouble on my very first day back in school," she said, gritting her teeth in mock rage.

I shot her a sarcastic look, with which I caught her eye.

She rolled her eyes and yielded with a shrug. "It's been several hundred years, okay? Give me a break."

Though her eyes pleaded with me for respite, I rolled my own at her manufactured drama and said, "Whatever." Then under my breath, "Immortals complaining about immortality."

"I heard that," she said.

"Duh," I said, pointing at both of us, "immortal." I couldn't concentrate on math for anything. If the president of the United States were to suddenly walk into the room in a clown suit with a gift pony as a bribe for my attention, I still wouldn't have been able to stop staring at Ellie. She was alive. And here. I wanted so badly to know what was going on.

"Relax, girlie. You look good, by the way, and I'm glad you made it home in one piece," I heard inside my head.

Can you hear me? I asked her. No response. I sighed, exasperated.

I looked over at her one last time and saw a smirk on her face. I was going to have to wait for the answers I wanted, and she was teasing me.

"HEY, HANDSOME."

Michael closed his locker and leaned against the door, taking

my arm and pulling me to his chest. He kissed me and held me. I
felt my shoulders relax. Something about his touch made me forget
all the things that were stressing me out. "You smell good. And have
I mentioned that you're kind of awesome?"

Pushing back so I could see his face, he winked and nodded.
"Yeah, I kind of am."

We both laughed and it felt good to feel … good.

"I see Ellie's back. Have you talked to her? Where's Kreios?"

"Easy, mister. She's been putting me off a little because of
classes, but I'm meeting her in a few minutes." I had been Michael's
ride to school that morning and I was planning to take Ellie home,
so I asked and made sure he had a ride home.

"Sure, I'll find a ride. I have football practice anyway. You
know, with state in our reach, everyone's getting excited."

"I know. It's annoying." All anyone could talk about was going
to state, and the last thing I cared about was high school football.
"Come by later?"

Michael smirked and got that boyish look in his eye that I
loved. "Miss me, huh? I'll text you when I'm done with practice.
You find out what you can from Ellie." He kissed me on the cheek
and left me standing there feeling a little sad that we wouldn't be
with each other on the way home. I'd grown used to having him
around and couldn't help but worry a little when he was off alone.

I walked to my car and crammed my bag into the trunk.

Normally when school was out, I would meet up with Kim, and
we would chit-chat and banter our way to my trusty Honda, and
then chit-chat and banter our way to my house, where we'd chit-
chat and banter our way through our homework. And maybe even a
TV show.

But not now. Not ever again. I shook the dark thoughts away,
but I still couldn't shake this deep sadness I felt in my core.

"Hey, Airel."

I looked up to behold an electric blue poof. Under it, a face I had come to love. Ellie. *My, er... grandma.* Family. Without any warning, I crumbled under an emotional avalanche. I fell into her arms and started crying like a complete fool.

I had lots of reasons to be a blubbering mess. The fact that my boyfriend, whom I loved more than my own life, wasn't around in my time of need, that I knew I wouldn't see him for the rest of the day. That my Kimmie was gone forever, that my parents had turned into dictators and imposed a curfew on my social life. That the idea of a social life for me was a total joke anyway. I cried for all this and more. Holding on to Ellie meant I was safe somehow, that what had happened to me was real, that everything was going to be okay because she was alive.

Thankfully Ellie didn't laugh at me or shove me away. She held me and let me cry it out. How weird was it that from the outside, she looked like another freaky girl in high school, while inside, in truth, she was the direct descendant of an angel of El, *the* angel of El, and that she was—what—about 3,263 years old?

I eventually calmed myself. "Sorry," I said, wiping my eyes and standing back.

"You ruined my favorite shirt," she said. But her tone was full of compassion. "You all right?"

"Yeah," I had to laugh at myself and shake my head. "Jeez. I'm such a girl."

She shrugged. "Better than being a boy. Imagine all that body hair and the smell … ugh." I snickered and she took my arm. "So, I don't want to be a bother or anything, but I don't have a place to stay. Or a car."

"Hmm, that is a problem. Whatever shall you do?" I said, pretending to be aloof. "Where do you want to go?"

"Your place."

"Really. I hear there are some nice rooms at the Hilton Garden Inn." I was being a little mean, but she had it coming.

"What, you think I'm rich or something?" She winked. "I'm here to stay. Now that I've found you, I'm not gonna let you out of my sight. I've much to teach you, grasshopper."

"Psh," I scoffed. "What's your story, though? I mean, for my parents?"

"Oh, I'm sure I can come up with something."

I thought for a second myself. "You're gonna need a place to stay besides Kim's old room …" I caught myself sinking down into grief again, but propelled myself out of it. "Hey."

"What?" She tossed her bag in the back.

"Just what do I call you? I mean, are you Uriel or Eriel or—"

She grinned. "I think Ellie's the least confusing for everyone, don't you? Besides, I've grown to like it." She got in on the passenger side.

I smiled. She would always be Ellie to me anyway, and that was all that counted right then and there. I slid in behind the wheel. "Sounds good to me, Ellie."

"Now, mate, who is the stud with the raven hair? He was totally checking you out."

CHAPTER XI

Glasgow, Scotland—Present Day

JORDAN WESTON CALLED THE boardroom to order, motioning to the others to sit.

Rain fell outside. It was a thoroughly Scottish December day, which wasn't surprising at all.

The modern and thick floor-to-ceiling panes of glass that separated the Glaswegian weather from the boardroom and its sharp-edged wood slab conference table were also normal, unsurprising.

The gathering of the board of directors too was *de rigeur.*

What was surprising, though, *in extremis,* was the packet of papers Jordan held in his good hand. Rather, the information they contained that had precipitated the meeting. That was what was surprising.

Why? It was obvious.

Jordan felt the dull, aching pain in his un-good hand, the left one, and thought for the millionth time how ironic it was that he had to headquarter here in Glasgow, with the precise variety of prevailing atmospheric conditions that produced pain in the withered hand. Nature had a sense of humor, and it was wicked. But it was Glasgow or nothing. Of all the thin places in the world under the sun, this one was perhaps the thinnest and therefore one of the most powerful. *Celts and Stonehenge and ... and on and on, that's why.*

He rubbed his left hand with his right and thought absently of healing as he spoke. "Blaise, kindly shut the doors."

A pear-shaped bespectacled man in tweed near the doors rose and closed them.

Jordan—this was the name by which he was known here— leaned back in his executive chair, a sleek thing made of polished aluminum and woven black fibers and plastics that were better than the finest steel. He looked out at the rain from five floors up, over the roofs of most neighboring buildings, into the fog.

Blaise sat at the table again.

"News from South Africa," Jordan said, taking up the packet of papers. "The Nri have been scattered." He assessed the reaction around the table. It was considerable. "Quite possibly, they have fallen altogether. Nwaba has been eternally bound."

Megan Combes, a fiftyish matronly woman in a suit as gray as the average leaded Scottish day, spoke. "The second death." She sounded as if someone had ruined her home-baked cake.

Old red-faced Charles Brant, an aristocratic throwback whose head was crowned with an unattractive and unruly explosion of brown hair, said as much to her as to anybody else, "It's not possible."

Others around the table spoke, saying, "Vicious lies," and "But the Nri are one of the Original Clans," and so on. Disbelief was the tying thread.

"Believe it," Jordan said. He raised the papers up. "Pass this packet around. All the information is here." He pushed back from the table, stood, and walked to the glass wall, looking out, watching the raindrops as they beaded on the other side of the glass, running downward. "Some of you may need to renew your reading of the Book of the Brotherhood, refresh your knowledge of the angel Kreios. The angel of El."

"Cursed," the group said as one, pronouncing the word in two syllables.

"Kreios has reappeared." The board was silent, and he assumed their silence signified shock and surprise, if not at least healthy respect for their mutual foe. "But that is not all. There have been other developments."

Jordan Weston turned to face them. "The heir, the Alexander, is lost. Perhaps temporarily, perhaps irrevocably—it will depend upon his choices now. The Stone is therefore loose; it seeks the final line. And more. There is … There has occurred an unforeseen event. There is another immortal, freshly activated. A girl. Her name is Airel. She possesses power unlike we have seen since the first age, our Dawning, and it grows daily. It is suspected that she will surpass even Kreios." His eyes widened and then he revised his statement. "If she has not already."

It took a moment for the import of this statement to sink in.

Charles spoke once more. "What shall we do?"

Jordan clasped his un-good hand in his good hand behind him and rocked forward and back, flexing his calves. "I feel we should discuss strategy. That is why we're assembled in this capacity— talking of the Real, and not our cover business."

"Very well," Blaise said. "I propose we send you," he looked at Jordan, "to consult with the Infernals."

"I've already taken the liberty," Jordan replied, "given the seriousness of the situation. I should like to do you one better, though." The tone around the table was as if they were merely discussing the results of an election for town council. "I should like to inquire in regard to the insertion of a specialist."

"Speak clearly now," Megan said. "Do you mean to call up one from the Garrison of the Offspring?"

"It would be a similar billet to that of Kasdeja," Jordan said.

"An infiltrator," Charles said, and then fell silent in thought for a moment. "Would it work as well the second time round?"

Jordan smiled. "They call him Valac," he corrected. "And yes. This one is very, *very* good. But not just good—smart. In the past, we have put too much stock in raw talent. One needs hunger, a drive, a taste for this sort of thing. And besides, not all signs point to the Alexander as the rightful heir. I believe there is another."

It was a rare thing indeed to be able to find one of the Brotherhood who did not drain the cursed. The one defense they had was that they could feel danger before it got close enough to strike, but not this time. This time, the girl Airel would not escape so easily.

CHAPTER XII

In the northeastern mountains of Turkey—Present Day

KREIOS LANDED ON THE outskirts of town and smoothed his
hair. It was longer now, as it had been quite some time since his last
haircut. He moved easy down the dirt road, wondering if the cursed
man he sought was still alive. He suspected yes, or the Books were
wrong.

They were never wrong.

After a mile's walk, he came upon a one-room house of stone,
mostly dug out of the earth and fashioned from rocks that had been
taken from the two fields behind it.

According to the Books, the man had taken no wife, and there
were no children. There was no family, there were no forebears
or ancestors left. There was no legacy but the earth and what the
cursed man put into it—his toil, his sweat—and what he took from
it—the harvest it gave him.

The farmer, an old man, lived like a soldier might. His
conquests were not those that would spill blood—not anymore—but
rather over the terrain itself. He was on his own out here in this
wasteland. If he could not work, he would not eat. All he had was

what he could grow. Kreios found a spot to sit under an old oak tree overlooking the solitary farm. He watched as the man stepped from the porch to begin his day. He looked at the man's hands. They were rough and weather-beaten, perpetually etched with dirt. Kreios hoped that his long life had been filled with misery and pain. If any of El's creatures deserved that, this man did.

He moved slowly toward his fields like a rusty hinge hanging on an old door, paying the angel of El no mind. Kreios wasn't sure if he was being ignored or if the man was simply that dull.

Kreios saw the goats. There were six of them, each with a tin bell that clanked like small voices from a different world. The man walked amongst the herd, rubbing his eyes and running his fingers through his short-cropped hair, gingerly probing the mark on his forehead. Still there, Kreios saw. Still unhealed after all these years. Kreios grunted in satisfaction; this was indeed the man he sought. He pulled a pouch from his coat and rolled himself a cigarette.

The man grasped a hoe that was leaning against the wall and walked toward a small patch of tilled earth to the side of the house. The sun was still low, concealed by the ridge to the south, and gray low-slung clouds in the interim carried snow with them. "Another day," he said and began working, hoeing out by the roots buckets of dormant floral grasses for the goats.

Kreios spent the next little while watching, thinking of what he would do with the cursed man. A plan was working in the deep parts of his mind, but it was not yet fully formed. Kreios knew that the Bloodstone was moving; soon a new Seer would emerge. He would need to be ready to strike before that happened.

The man walked over to the goat pen and threw the weeds and grasses on the ground in the middle. He used the bucket to fetch water from the well. Then he tended to his modest winter crop of beets, garlic, and potatoes, planted up against the wall of his house for at least a little shelter.

As the man worked, Kreios found his thoughts turning toward the ancient peoples. Where the man lived was not far from the Kara Su, what others might call the Western Euphrates, high above where it joined the Murat Su, the Eastern Euphrates, and then became one river. It was a high region of forest and brush far from where mankind had first trod the earth. Far from the garden that was now guarded by the angel of El with the flashing sword.

Here in the mountains by the Kara Su, the man was far from his old life, the past he had long ago fled. He was far from the mountains of Hijaz, where he had killed his brother.

CHAPTER XIII

Boise, Idaho—Present Day

WE STOPPED OFF AT my favorite coffee shop. It was the very same Moxie Java where, really, this whole thing had started. I ordered my "yooszh," which was a coconut latté, only this time as a decaf. I was buzzed already, and didn't need the jitters. Ellie ordered a cup of Earl Grey and we sat by the fire and sipped and talked.

"So," she said, "how about you and the new guy, Dirk … What will Michael think? What a scandal."

"Haha," I said, "laugh it up."

"Once upon a time, Michael was that new guy."

"Hey, don't be mean. If you think Dirk's so hot, you date him."

"Don't be nasty. He's hundreds of years younger than I am." She giggled. "So … you're probably amazed I'm alive."

"Um, yeah." I felt I should try to keep my interjections to a minimum for now, but I couldn't resist asking where in the high heels she had been for the last few months.

She sighed, visibly heavy. "You probably ought to know a few things about me before I start bringing you up to speed. First, if you must know, I've been staying up at my father's place."

"You mean …"

"Yeah. Under the waterfall and all that."

I chuckled darkly. "Narnia."

"Pretty much. I had a lot of things to do there. A lot of studying. But anyway, I need to start my story elsewhere. You've read up on Uncle Yamanu, yes?"

I nodded, sipping, my eyes locked on her over the top of my cup.

"So you're familiar with the shadowing arts."

"Yes."

"And how far did the Book of Kreios permit you to read?"

"What do you mean? I read that book to the end. Many times."

She smiled. "No, girlie. You read it to the end it allowed you to see. So … how far did you get, then?"

"I …" I had to think. I was stunned at this new development. "I think it was before Christ still. Seven hundred B.C. somewhere, I guess." I closed my eyes and tried to remember specifics. "788, I think."

Her smirk turned, betraying unmistakable pain. "You don't know even half, then."

I couldn't do anything but sit and stare.

"If you're wondering why the Book did that to you, don't. It was for your own protection. If fallible creatures of free will knew where their choices were to take them, they would become enslaved to inevitability. El has far greater love than to show us all ends."

She sounded like an old woman, but it was hard to look at her and her blue hair and hear the way she could slip into wise old woman talk. "So what did I miss?" I asked.

She took a sip of her tea, savoring it. "The shadowers." She sighed. "Yamanu knew I had been activated by the time I arrived at the City of Refuge. I have no doubt he prayed to El about it, that he ultimately received confirmation that he should train me as a shadower anyhow. I don't know why, but he did. It only took one lesson for me to surpass him in every way. The rest, I learned on my own through trial and error."

She looked out the window for a second and then let her gaze come to rest on the flames behind the glass in the fireplace. "I made a lot of errors. But in the end, I came up solid. I learned new ways to practice the art. Yamanu was a powerful master. He was able to call up the shadows in a physical fog, he was able to counteract the drain our kind feel around the Bloodstone, around the Brotherhood.

"As I came to maturity—and it takes years, girlie, trust me—I felt my gift increasing, doubling in power again and again. See, no one knows how our kind, the half-breed kind, will fully manifest upon activation. Anything could happen. Any power might be gifted, brought into this realm from the eternal. This is why the Brotherhood are so bent on rooting us out by intentionally activating us and then killing us. Because they don't know how powerful we'll turn out as individuals, Airel, and that scares them.

"The truth of the matter is that mankind wasn't made a little lower than the *angels*. Mankind was made a little lower than *El,* at least before the Fall. Psalm eight."

I shook my head. "I don't have it memorized. Do I look like a Bible scholar?"

"My point is," she continued, "when the blood of mortal women was mixed with that of our fallen fathers in their resultant children together, what occurred was not a perversion of angelic purity. It was an augmentation of potential power, because mankind was made in the image of El. The one-third that follows the Day Star, Lucifer, know this and hate it and seek to suppress the truth so we will cower in submission before them.

"Further, they know that with each passing day after activation, our power and gifting only grows. That was the case for me. It has been the case for you as well."

I had to agree with her. At first, I had been a retching basket case. Through my own trial and error, plus the training Kreios had given me, I grew in power every time I overcame. Heck, I had even wielded the Sword of Light. *Though not lately. Not even when I try like crazy to call it up.* I guessed it had something to do with the universe of things I had yet to understand.

She sipped her tea again and then continued. "My gift isn't so much to call up a shadow or fog. No, it's different with me. I guess it's just El showing his sense of humor. My gift is that I become one *with* the shadow. I can disperse myself into the air at will. I guess you could say that for all intents and purposes, I can disappear into thin air.

"The first time I did it, I thought I'd died. But I concentrated very hard on bringing myself back together, and succeeded. After that, it was simply a matter of courage and practice.

"I mention all of this for a reason, Airel. You remember that conversation we had on the island? With the seals?"

"Seal Island," I said. "How could I forget? You told me to swim naked."

"I was right, naturally."

I blushed and shrugged. "Mostly."

"You do remember what you said to me before you dove in, right?"

"Yeah. I asked you to help Michael."

"And I said I would do all I could, didn't I?"

My mind flashed back. *Yes. That was precisely what she'd said.* I didn't answer aloud. I felt like my world was about to get rocked once again and I didn't want to speak.

"I did all I could," she said. "When you jumped into False Bay, you did it selflessly. You demonstrated to me total lack of fear. Sure, some of it was ignorance because you didn't know how fierce and bloodthirsty those sharks could be in that area—but you did it. You committed your body to the deep, for love. You . . . It was an act of bold faith, Airel. You may as well have walked on water, for all the difference it would have made to me."

"What are you saying, Ellie?"

"I'm saying you inspired me to use extreme measures, to take action. And I did what I was able to do. Did you never wonder how the Mark passed from Michael to me?"

"Well, yes," I said. "But I—Michael and I both figured you just, you know, had your ways. Or that El intervened somehow. Then again, this is the first time I've seen you in months."

She nodded. "I took the Mark upon myself because my unique shadowing abilities allowed me to physically dissolve not only myself, but also *it*. The Mark. I, well, for lack of a better word, I tricked it into clinging to me, into letting Michael go."

"But how?"

"What, are you asking for a demonstration right here?"

I looked around us. "No," I hissed, feeling the need to lower my voice. "But what happened next? How did you get off the island? And what about Kreios? What about all that happened up on Table Mountain?"

"My shadowing abilities have grown very strong, Airel. But it all changed when you did what you did. I could always teleport, for lack of a better word—but not very far. The longer I am in the wind, the harder it is to get all the pieces back together again."

"Wait. You're telling me that you tried to teleport off the island? With Michael? You could have killed him. What if your stuff and his stuff got all mixed up?" My head was starting to hurt.

"Like I said, I felt like I had to try. For all I knew, you were going to drown, and I couldn't risk Michael dying there on my watch. Even without the Mark, he was not going to do well. Anyway, I tested it out." Her eyes met mine, and I could tell she was about to confess something to me. "The first few times, we ended up in the middle of the ocean. But the third time, we made it."

"This is crazy. *You're* crazy. You know that, right?"

"Depends on your definition of 'crazy'. All I know is that it worked. And I've been testing myself ever since."

"And Kreios—is he … dead?"

"I don't know, Airel. He is preeminent among angels, so I want to believe he made it somehow. When I woke up after he did whatever he did, I was all alone." For the first time since Ellie had been back, the ready wit she wore like armor fell away. She bit her lip, and I saw tears nearing the surface.

"So he took the Mark for you?"

Ellie nodded and stared at her tea.

I reached out and touched her hand. She lifted her head and managed a smile. "But like I said, he is more powerful than any of us—for now, anyway."

"What's that mean?"

Ellie cocked her eyebrow and her snarky demeanor returned. "It means that your grandfather is the Angel of Death. Read up on what happened to Egypt when Pharaoh crossed El and lost every single Egyptian firstborn. Read up on the Jewish Passover feast and what it means. Read up on what happened at the ancient city-state of Ai. For that matter, read up on what happened at that petrochemical skyscraper in Cape Town, how many people simply vanished the night before you saw him in the sky and flew to him. Read up on how there were random piles of sand on every floor, how each one weighed what an average man might weigh if every trace of water in him had spontaneously evaporated. *All* Kreios. Airel, do you have any idea what it's like growing up when your father is El's ambassador for the grave? You think you and *your* dad have issues."

I shook my head, wide-eyed. "So …"

"So Kreios is out-of-this-world powerful. When he sets his mind to something, *especially* when El is directly involved, nothing is impossible for him."

"Then he has to be alive." I wanted so badly for it to be true, and I could tell Ellie needed to believe it as well so she could at least have one last hope left to hold on to.

"Yeah, I think so," she said. "If anyone can make it through what he had to go through, it's him." She took a sip of her tea, swallowed it slowly, and then breathed in the steamy aroma through her nostrils.

She looked as if she was enjoying it even more than I loved my coconut latté. I thought about trying Earl Grey sometime. She made it look pretty dang yummy. "So," I asked, trying not to cry for Kreios, *which is weird because it seems like he can handle himself,* "what happened to him? I mean, when he took the Mark?"

"That's what I've been trying to find out. I've read all the books I could get my hands on at his place to see if there are any answers. The ones I found weren't pretty."

I breathed out. "This is a lot to process." I leaned forward and buried my face into the heels of my palms and rubbed my eyes, took a deep breath or two, and then leaned back in my chair. "But what now? What do *we* do? What happens to us? Are we safe? Where's Kreios?"

Ellie laughed and shook her head. "He will show himself when he wants to be seen. When he's able. For now, we stick to our cover and keep our noses in our books. Got it?"

"Sure," I said, aghast at how the entirety of my high school career had just been upended because of this tiny change in perspective. *Being a student is my cover now?* I wanted to believe that Kreios was alive, but when I reached out for him, I got nothing. This wasn't the first time I hadn't been able to feel him, but I still worried.

"You'll have lots more questions. Ask them. Just be careful when and where. Pretend the walls have eyes and ears, 'kay?"

I agreed with a glance. Outside, the first snow of the season was falling. I wondered if it would stick or just make the roads a mess. I grabbed my drink for a sip of coconutty goodness, but it was empty. I looked outside at the cold, the wet snow, and then at Ellie. "I think I want to try some of that tea."

She smiled. I was glad indeed to have her back, even though, in truth, I felt as empty as my coffee cup.

CHAPTER XIV

Arabia—926 B.C.

"WHERE IS THE BLOODSTONE, Daughter of Death?"

Uriel appeared before Anael draped in a dark gray cloak that reached her toes. "Lost, destroyed, no longer in these realms—who can say? I hunt it day and night, but I have yet to locate its possessor."

Anael cursed her in the forbidden tongue. She could feel both his anger and his fear. He was right to fear her—she had grown much more powerful now. Surely he had heard rumors—if he hadn't, he was not a worthy adversary.

"You have failed me. Our pact is now at an end." His voice was tense and he clenched his fists.

"Why so rash, old man? I have only failed if I find the stone and then fail to hand it over to you. What, is your trust so short-lived? And do you think it an easy thing that I should go and steal this trinket for you? Without me, you have no hope of finding it, and even if by dumb luck you do, who will go in and wrench it away from its host? Not you. You could not surprise a deaf man from behind."

Anael snarled and made a grab for the hilt of his sword, but Uriel moved like lightning, taking it from him before his fingers touched it. She stood back, holding it out before him as if she had never moved.

The change was immediate. "Please," Anael said, falling to his knees.

Uriel crinkled her nose in disgust. "Do I need to rid the world of yet another coward?" She stuck the tip of the sword into the ground and approached him, crouching down just out of his reach. "What do they say of me?"

Anael shifted his weight and avoided her eyes.

She grasped his cloak and forced him to meet her eyes. "What do they say?"

"They call you the Derakhshan, meaning the bright, the light before death."

She stood, crossing her arms and nodding. "And?"

"They say you live in the wind, that you appear to heat-crazed, exhausted travelers in the deserts in the hot brilliance of the day, shimmering over superheated sands. They hear your voice in their heads; they say you drive men mad. You strike terror into men's hearts, melting their courage like wax."

Uriel sighed in confirmation. This was even better news than that which she had heard among the Scythians to the north. "And what of you, Anael? What do you believe?"

He hesitated, but she could see a smirk brewing at the corners of his mouth. "I believe you are not one to go back on your word … that you honor your father with all you do." He spit it out like an accusation.

Uriel flared in anger, and black mist boiled from her robes. Before Anael could react, she brandished the edge of his sword at his throat. "You dare mock me, impotent old man? Throwing my father into my face? Once, I let it go unpunished. Shall I suffer further insult from you now?" She threw him to the ground.

An instant later, she was gone, having moved to the top of one of the high towers in the City of Refuge. She would not hear of her father, *would not,* because deep within her heart she harbored regret for the way things ended. *But he killed the man I loved.* Pathways to revenge remained open and inviting. In fact, they were irresistible, and every time she thought of Kreios, she tasted blood.

Uriel scanned the city from her perch, trying to calm herself. *The pact.* Stealing the Bloodstone would not be easy; the task had proven itself to be so. It seemed nothing in her life would be easy— nothing would bring her the peace she craved. She remembered her friends, her young adventures, and wondered if life would ever be like that again.

Doubtful.

She was one of the Brotherhood now. She was not a slave like most; they gave her a long leash. *The Infernals know that one such as I will not be controlled.* The acting Seer might have made her an Infernal, given her skill. But she had no desire to command a regular unit of troops. Uriel's heart was made of and for things other than intoxication with mere power. Those things could never satisfy her.

Part of her—a part she could resist less and less as the days dragged on—longed for understanding, for companionship. She began to fantasize about walking into a marketplace like a normal human being might do, seeing those sights, letting those sounds and smells bounce off her fully manifest form. On occasion, she had. She told herself she was working, that she was in disguise and gathering information that could be used elsewhere. But the truth was, she wasn't *working.* She wasn't gathering information, wasn't acting in a tactical sense at all. She was feeding her needs.

Below in the city, she could hear Yamanu, and Veridon's booming voice, her uncle Zedkiel. She listened to the angelic peoples of the city indulging in dead memories. But the longer she listened, the more pain she could feel—El. And the men who had taught her to worship Him. Who was El to her? To the Derakhshan? El was a light trick, a rumor. El was nothing but the god of her father, the god of her people—and these had betrayed her.

Enraged, she stood and took to the air. Tonight she would fly. It would feel like the old days for a few dark hours.

She could not fly away, however, from the one thing that caused her heart to beat now. And Anael had stirred it to action. She wanted only one thing. Only this could bring her peace and fulfillment—causing this city to fall.

CHAPTER XV

Zurich, Switzerland—Present Day

FRANK HAD DEPLANED IN Zurich a little baffled. Emerald had gone—he couldn't find her. It wasn't as if he could risk waiting around for her to walk out of the loo or wherever she'd gotten off to. While it was disappointing, Frank reasoned that he had bigger fish to fry on this bright and sunny day.

The buyer, for one. What any fool would want with an old book stuffed with nothing but blank pages was beyond him. *Well, they weren't all blank, were they? There was that very last page, wasn't there?* "But she lived," Frank said aloud, driving his freshly hired full-size Merc on the wrong side of the road, and on the wrong side of the car, for that matter.

He chuckled as a low sun in a northern hemisphere winter crested the Alps and began to sparkle off Lake Zurich. Life was quirky. "But she lived," he said again, and he wondered who "she" was. "Perhaps her name is that word I heard on the beach there," he said, "when I first picked the book up." *But what was that word? Heiress? No. It was something else.*

Frank Wiseman parked the car along the curb of a street that started with the letter G and got out, scanning at the slip of paper in his fat fingers. He read the address and looked around at the building numbers for confirmation. It was not the worst part of town, but then again, this was Switzerland. There were no bad parts. Such things the Swiss did not allow.

There. "Building two, number seventeen, G Street." It was actually *Gasstrasse,* but who cared. It was a neighborhood of multistory walkups, flats where people either lived or did business, the odd dance studio or naturopathic doctor's office. *Or book buyer.* Frank wasn't sure if he ought to suspect a proper bookshop or a private residence when he rang the bell.

There came from within a muffled Swiss-German reply. Friendly. Bidding him to be patient, probably. He adjusted his overcoat around his body, checked the pocket—the Stone was there—and clasped his hands together over the book in front of him, looking up at the door, anticipating the face he would see when it opened.

"Well, isn't this a pleasant surprise." Emerald Ruby, the woman he lusted after, stood in the doorway in a painted-on red dress.

A ruby dress. "I say. Fate has smiled upon us, dear girl. You look amazing, as ever." Frank felt his blood stir and something in him made whispers from long-forgotten places.

"Thank you, Mr. Wiseman. And what should bring you to my door? Oh, wait. Don't tell me. Are you my appointment?" She ran her finger down the bare skin of her neck and let it linger low in the V of her dress.

Frank had to force himself from the trance in which he found himself. She was beautiful ... *well, not beautiful, but sexy . . .* but she was far too young for him. "I am indeed the seller. You must be the buyer I've heard so much about. I never imagined . . . but why do you work as an airline stewardess?"

She stepped aside, inviting him in. "Rare books are not as profitable as one might think, Mr. Wiseman. And technically, I work *with* the buyer. You can call me his secretary."

Frank stepped inside the dimly lit entry, breathing in the bouquet of her scent as he passed by. *She smells like honey and . . . and . . .*

The door slammed shut and something tore behind him. He smiled, allowing his imagination to run wild. *She wants me so bad, she tore her own dress off.* As he turned around, he saw that he was only half right.

Frank had no time to scream as her barbed tail whipped around, slicing him across the face. Blood splattered the wall, he dropped the book, and it landed at her feet.

"Now we get to play," she said. "Do you like to play, Frankie boy? I do. My momma used to tell me not to play with my food, but I showed her."

Frank couldn't find words for what he now saw. The superhuman strength for which he had cultured a taste left him. He fell to his knees, soiling his pants.

The demon slithered free from Emerald's body, and she staggered half naked into another room.

Black goo dripped from rows of long fangs. The monster spread out one wing and then another, balancing itself. "You have done well, pawn." The demon's voice was like gravel, and as its hot breath blasted Frank's face, he understood that this was all the thanks he would receive. He trembled, trying to stand, but the demon grasped him bodily in one pincer, ripping him in half at the waist. Frank was aware of the pain. He was aware of the shock. He was aware of his feelings that this kind of treatment was unfair to him. His thoughts briefly condemned him with one word— *Kimberley.* But the pain was too intense.

And the Bloodstone was free. Frank could see it on the floor on the opposite side of the room. By his legs.

The demon picked up his bloody legs, popped them into his mouth, and crunched. Blood smeared his teeth and gushed down, splattering on the floor.

The Bloodstone hummed on the floor in front of the beast. It was calling now not to Frank, but to the beast—it wanted to belong to another.

So the beast took it and then finished his meal.

THE THREE ANTICHERUBIM MANIFESTED in the present day, in the darkness of a desert night in Arabia, the moon above merely a discarded fingernail clipping, cast among cursedly sparkling crumbs of the detritus of the sky. The three crawled up from the pit of a thin place into the blinding light of a black night, the stars set like jewels in a veil of ink above. This was the veil El had drawn to hide himself from those creatures he had made to dwell under the sun. Beauty is hatred; hatred is beauty, they thought together, and then the larger one stopped and twisted its neck around.

"The Bloodstone has been found. Two of us shall go as one, but you, Magi, must stay to guard this place." Green eyes flashed and with a flick of her tongue, Magi, the smallest of the three, obeyed without a word. She was the smallest, but by no means the weakest. In fact, she was faster and stronger than the others. There would be none better to guard the thin place, to keep any other creatures from coming through until the appointed time.

Magi watched the other two anticherubim as they turned west over the sands, seeking the assigned prince who would carry the Bloodstone into battle. They darted above the sand in spastic twitches, flitting like insects, and they were very fast. They would reach their destination very soon, the land where it all started, where the First Dawn had occurred in the First Age.

The mountains of Hijaz.

Where Eden once was.

On the way, their simple assignment was to gather the true heir and escort him to Hijaz, where the new Seer would be anointed with the blood of the Tree.

Among the many kingdoms of men on the earth, there were rulers who thought the honor of Seer would be theirs. But Magi's master was the only one who could lay claim in truth, though some there would be those who argued otherwise. The war for which the Brotherhood hungered was coming quickly; the people of the earth would be caught in the middle. But this world was rightfully Brotherhood territory. It was theirs in the beginning when man gave it over in the Garden. Mankind had been deceived for thousands of years, but the time was now here—the dawn of the chastening of man had come.

CHAPTER XVI

Boise, Idaho—Present Day

ONE THING I DECIDED—YEAH, Earl Grey's not my cup of tea. I wrinkled my nose.

Michael laughed. "That bad, huh?"

"Worse. Who would like this stuff? I mean, besides Ellie. She's weird, so that doesn't count."

"I like tea," Michael said, defending her even though she wasn't there. "A good black tea with honey in the morning can be quite refreshing."

"Ha. You two can have it. I can see why they tossed it overboard." We sat across from each other in the Cheesecake Factory. Michael wanted to take me out on a "date" and this was the first place he had ever taken me. But that awesome dress and that naïve life seemed like ages ago. I changed the subject. "So, how is your new foster family?"

Michael's eyes darkened and his bad mood returned. "Okay, I guess. I should leave—blow this town and live out on my own."

"I know, Michael," I said, touching his hand, "but we only need to make it to graduation. Then we can go together." Because

Michael was a minor, the State of Idaho had placed him with Child Protective Services until everything with his father got ironed out.

"I should have skipped out before the cops took all my stuff for evidence. Now I have nothing." He cursed. I still didn't understand what was going on and how they could do that to him.

"What is probate, anyway?" I asked.

"Who knows. It means I'm broke and have to put up with stupid foster parents." He made air quotes around this last word. Michael had been distant the past few weeks. I was trying to be supportive and understanding, but it was starting to get old. I had my own problems and *I* needed *him;* I didn't have much left to offer before my heart gave out. I could feel it.

He gave me his trademark half smile. "It'll be okay. Besides, you hear all the talk around school? Or the lack of talk—it's like I grew a third eye or something. Between the kidnapping, Kim's death, and my dad, we're the local freaks."

"Hey, that's not true." I knew it was, though; people avoided even making eye contact with me. I was glad I had Ellie to hang out with so I didn't look like a total loser.

"You know it is, Airel. Even the guys on the team are acting weird. I find out about parties the day after, and nobody talks to me anymore in the locker room even though I'm the guy who's getting us to state this year."

"Well, at least they found you a home in the same district so you didn't have to change schools. And you guys are killing it this year."

He seemed to brighten a little when I said that. Since they had "lost" James, their star quarterback, Coach Dennis offered the job to Michael and he filled in, doing better than James had ever done. In Michael's first start, our team beat Boise High 38-0. He passed *and* rushed for over a hundred yards each. And yeah, the quarterback's girlfriend can totally memorize the stats and brag on her guy. I had hoped his growing fame on the field would translate to the halls, but I wasn't so sure.

I listened to Michael talk shop, the different plays and all that. I let myself enjoy the moment. He was happy, and even if it would only last until the end of the conversation, I would take what I could get and hope he would get something out of it too.

It went without saying that Michael and I were important to each other, and that, in spite of my parents' wishes to the contrary, we were still together. It was also true that I loved him, but things were not the same between us. I had faith that things would get better eventually, but that got harder to believe every day. Mostly, I felt like I was the only one rooting for *us*. Every time I saw him, it was like he was less Michael and more something else. I worried that he was really depressed, that he wouldn't be able to pull himself out of it on his own. Worse, I didn't know how to help him.

"DON'T LOOK NOW, BUT guess who?" Ellie had her back to the long row of lockers and was fussing absentmindedly over her nails.

I dropped a book on purpose so I could see where her eyes were motioning without looking like a total idiot. It was Dirk Elliott, only a few feet away, staring in our direction. I turned back to Ellie. "He sure isn't shy about liking you," I whispered. "You should put him out of his misery and go talk to him."

Ellie rolled her eyes. "He likes you, not me, silly. Besides, I don't think he likes my blue hair."

"Not possible. How could he not like you? He's in a band, you're exotic ... it's a no-brainer." I shoved the rest of my books into my locker and slammed it shut. "Look into my eyes, Ellie. It's

Michael … me and Michael."

"You mean demon boy?"

I glared at her.

"Sorry … old habit." She sighed. "Fine, you and Michael, I'll be good." She tensed. "Um … oh, wait, uh, Airel."

"What? Is the hot hunk of a man standing behind me going to make me go all weak in the knees and fall all over myself for him?"

Someone cleared his throat behind me. I glared at Ellie and then spun around.

Dirk was standing there, smiling at me. He had one hand in his back pocket and the other was offering up the book I'd dropped.

"Oh, hi. Thanks." I grabbed the book and turned to face Ellie, glaring at her again "I think." I hoped she could read me loud and clear as I thought, *I am going to kill you as soon as I can.*

"My name's Dirk Elliott."

I turned back toward him. "Hi. How are you?" He offered his hand and I shook it, barely managing to keep from laughing out loud. "Here's the deal," I said, trying to begin to explain my *faux pas.* "I was just telling my friend here that all the girls think you're hot, that you'll have your pick of the litter."

Ellie shouldered her way next to me and chewed her gum in my ear. *Are you trying to be annoying?* "Hey, I'm Ellie. I'm glad to meet you. So, how's Boise compared to … where are you from again? It's some fruit, right?"

Dirk laughed. It was a nice laugh. "Orange County." He turned back to me and I felt uncomfortable with how he was looking at me. "What did you say your name was again?"

"I didn't, but it's Airel."

"Oh, like the mermaid?"

I groaned. "No, not like the mermaid. It's spelled A-i-r-e-l. Airel."

"Sorry. You must get that a lot."

"No, not really."

We all stood there as the other kids in the hall pretended not to be watching the whole thing. Ellie appeared to be enjoying the silence—the very awkward silence.

"So, I'm a drummer…" Dirk made the brave attempt to start up the conversation again. "I sing a little too, and my band has got this thing on Friday night at the District coffeehouse. I was thinking that since I have the—how did you put it? Pick of the litter?"

"Oh." I didn't like where this was going.

"Would you like to go to the show? We'll grab something to eat afterward."

"I have a boyfriend," I said.

"I know. Michael, right?"

"Uh, yeah." *Where's he going with this?*

"Bring him along," he said. "You should come too, Ellie. We need to pack the place out."

"Oh, I …" I felt stupid. *Am I not reading this guy right?*

Dirk went on. "I mean, I would much rather go with only you, Airel, but if I have to hang with your boyfriend in order to see more of that stunning face, so be it."

Stunned, I clamped my jaw shut. I wanted to slap him. But I smiled instead. "How do I say, 'No, not in a million years' in such a way that you'll never talk to me again?" My hands were warm. Kreios's training kicked right in; I remembered to hold back my anger so I wouldn't, you know, accidentally kill something or someone.

"Easy there. I was only asking," Dirk said, chuckling. "How could any guy not try? You're flat-out gorgeous. I mean, look at you." He smiled with a little too much charm and then walked away. He seemed like he had really thick skin—he wasn't flustered at all.

"Hmmm," Ellie said, "that went differently than I imagined it would."

I socked her in the arm. "You can shut it."

"What did I do?"

"You know what you did," I replied, even though it made no sense. I figured she would maybe guilt herself into remorse eventually.

Ellie giggled. "Yeah, I'll tell you what I'm *gonna* do. I'm gonna rethink my age difference rule." She swatted my butt. "Rawr."

I almost fell down laughing. Ellie was like my best friend lately. That realization hit me really hard because I had come upon it without my Kimmie. I didn't know if I should laugh or cry; there was only a wild sea of feelings. I wasn't sure I was going to be able to navigate it successfully. But as I looked at Ellie's face, as we laughed together about the dumbest stuff, I at least had hope.

THE WEEK BEFORE CHRISTMAS break on a Friday night, when we'd beaten Timberline, I waited for Michael outside the locker room after the game. I only had about a half an hour to get home before my curfew expired, but I didn't care. I cared about Michael. The night felt so good. We had won. Michael was the star of the victory, and I was his girl, and the lights were still on over the field. Wispy snow flurries swirled into these white-yellow cones of light from out of nowhere; they went from being invisible in the black to shimmering like tiny mirrors in the light, making me feel like I was in a fairy tale. I could see my breath. The grass of the field smelled rich and dense, and the night sky was a blanket that made the world feel very small.

All I wanted was to live in this moment, for this lush feeling of rightness, of safety, to never end.

Michael came walking out of the double doors smiling at me. "Hey."

"Hey, mister. Good game."

"Aw, thanks. I keep hearing people say how good I am."

"Well, yeah. How does it feel to be going to state?"

He shrugged, and I could tell that it probably felt hollow. For a lot of reasons. "You know what a Pyrrhic victory is?"

"Yeah," I said. "One that costs too much."

His eyes were rimmed with moisture, and the exhalation that came from his nose produced a cloud of vapor that quickly cooled and dissolved into the air. "Yeah. One that costs too much." He looked at me. "Airel." He pulled me closer.

I looked up at him. "Yes."

"I'm glad you're here."

"Me too."

Everyone else filtered out and went away, and then as the moment decayed into nearly an hour, the field lights turned off and the stars became visible high above. We held hands and walked around the field in the dark.

When I finally got home later that night, I was two hours late. I was grounded before I closed the front door behind me. I told my dad, "Fine. I'm going to bed."

I could see the anger and frustration all over his face. "You keep bucking me like this and you'll be confined to your room."

I stopped halfway up the stairs. "Only for a few more months, Dad," I replied. "Once I turn eighteen, I'm gone. You want to smother me into hating you? You're doing a bang-up job." I knew I had hurt him by how he flinched and looked away. But I was so mad! I was pissed that he was acting like an overbearing psycho father. I needed his support, not iron bars.

"Airel, I'm trying to keep you—you know what, never mind. Just go."

"Fine." I turned and ran up the stairs, holding the tears inside until my door closed. My life was supposed to be getting back to normal, not becoming a living hell.

ELLIE WAS GLAD THAT Airel convinced her parents to let her stay with them. The truth was that Airel was the kind of girl who could use a friend who was unafraid to speak with wisdom when she needed to hear it most.

And there was another reason Ellie wanted to stay close by.

She could intuit that Airel's father, John, was not what he claimed to be. It wasn't the average travelling salesman who could pull international diplomatic levers like that. She suspected something from the little she had seen in South Africa, but after doing her own digging, she was convinced that John had something to hide.

But what?

That was the question. It was about 1:30 a.m., and when the phone rang, Ellie woke instantly but lay in bed waiting. She could hear John's voice down the hall. She faded into the air, moving out of her room toward his office.

John sat in a high-backed chair, fiddling with a paperclip as he talked on the phone.

"Who's this?" He paused, twisting the paperclip between his fingers.

Ellie could see the recognition on his face. It wasn't a good thing.

He sighed. "Oh."

She could feel his foreboding—this was not a friend on the other end.

"When and where?" He paused to listen.

"Okay," John said to the empty space. He placed the phone back in its cradle and opened his laptop.

Ellie moved around behind him and watched as he signed into his accounts, making sure she memorized his password in case she needed it later. *Looks like we're going on a little trip. Where to this time, John? I hope it's somewhere tropical. I could use a little base tan.*

And then John spoke again, this time to nobody. "I wonder if I'll be home for Christmas this year." He paused. "Something tells me no."

CHAPTER XVII

In the northeastern mountains of Turkey—Present Day

WHEN KREIOS AWOKE THE next day, he knew something was going to change forever. The winds were different. Not better or worse—just different. They brought with them the scent of something terrible. It was death, a thing Kreios knew how to wear when El allowed it.

Yes, everything would change today.

He made ready and soon sat on the ground before the hut of the man with the mark. An hour passed. He heard a stir inside, so he sat up a little straighter.

The man poked his head out from the flap of his front door. He did not visibly react to Kreios's presence. Maybe strange men had appeared to him before. The man's eyes were different from any Kreios had ever seen. They were all white, and the tiny pupils were not couched in irises, making them appear like pebbles pierced by deep blackness at the center. "Who are you?" the farmer asked.

"You know who I am, Cain."

The farmer emerged from his house and stood erect before the visitor. "You know that name?"

Kreios stood, easily doubling him for mass and size, standing at least two heads taller than Cain. "I do."

"Then you can only be the Angel of El." Cain bowed his head before Kreios. "What can I give to the Messenger of God?"

"Cain, the end draws close. The time has come for the father of murder under the sun to fulfill both his days and his call. El has a purpose for the mark you bear that you have not foreseen, though you have seen many years indeed."

Cain seemed pleased. He smiled and bowed again. "Only say the word, and I shall do what you command."

Kreios gestured to him. "Come with me to the nearest of the thin places—I seek to go where only you can take me."

Cain backed up a step and shook his head. "No. I will never go there, not ever again unless it is in death." Fear flooded his face, and Kreios began to glow. His tattoos burned bright and Cain quivered.

"You will take me now or you shall suffer for another thousand years, Cain. I am the taker of lives, and I shall forget you were ever born unless you do as I command."

Still Cain refused.

Kreios shrugged. "Very well. May you live long and be full of years. When I return to you in a thousand years, you will run to me with outstretched arms and beg me to allow you to do your duty." Turning, Kreios began to walk away. He was not surprised, though, when Cain called after him.

"Please, wait. Angel of El, I will go. Only swear to me that you will end my life once I take you to that place of torment."

Kreios stopped. He nodded without turning. "You will have rest from this life, this I swear."

Cain hobbled up to Kreios's side and they walked together into the forest. At the edge of the meadow, they disappeared.

Boise, Idaho—Present Day

AFTER A TOUGH DAY at school—one of those days that feel like nothing goes right and there's no explanation why—I went home, did my homework, streamed a couple of shows, and went to bed, falling asleep instantly.

I dreamed I was walking along a dusty trail. There were hoofprints and primitive wheel tracks in the powdery earth, and above me the sky looked unsettled, angry—rain was coming. I looked ahead and saw three black birds circling high, riding the updrafts.

As it usually happens in dreams, I didn't have to travel long to arrive. I was suddenly there, standing at the place where the birds were circling. I looked down.

I stood over a corpse.

The three black birds continued to circle overhead. I looked out to the horizon and saw pinpricks of black in the washed-out sky, standing out against snarling gray-black clouds, flying toward me. More vultures were gathering.

A part of me wanted to run, leave the body alone, but I wanted to see who it was. More birds swarmed and now they were diving low, trying to get me to leave their meal alone. I leaned down and rolled the body over so I could see its face.

It was me.

I screamed and sat up, finding myself at home in my own bed. It was dark out—the middle of the night, according to the clock on the nightstand. These nightmares were coming on stronger lately, more often too, and I felt it was *She* letting me know that something was coming.

"But what?" I asked the air. *She* didn't respond, as was her normal way. Our minds were almost one now, her voice almost my own. I liked having her for my sixth sense, but I needed some answers, not more riddles in the dark. I was sick of those. First it had been Kreios, and now *She*. When would my oppressions end?

I got up and started down the stairs to get a warm glass of milk, making sure not to wake Ellie, who was staying in Kim's old room. I was at the bottom of the stairs when I heard the phone ring. I could hear Dad talking in his office and I reached out to try to hear what he was saying. There was nothing, so I crept closer to the door and eavesdropped.

"Okay," he said. He sounded sad, as if whatever the news was, it was bad. I could see his back and part of his desk through the small space between the office door and the jamb. He opened his laptop, and in a moment had an email message up on the screen. I could make out an itinerary for airline tickets. At the top of the screen, I saw the CIA logo.

My body tensed. Some things started to fall into place in my head—others made no sense at all. *What is my dad doing, getting airline tickets from the CIA?*

Have you ever kissed in the rain?

Who is this?

It would be a shame never to kiss in the rain. This is Dirk.

How did you get my number?

I have my ways.

And I have a boyfriend.

So you keep telling me. Why didn't you go to my gig? It was packed. I searched the crowd for you and had to leave

disappointed.

**You will live a life of constant disappointment if you keep
chasing things you can't have.**

I don't want to possess you—I only want to be your friend.

You want more than that.

**I'm not texting you for an argument. Anyway, never mind
what I want. I'll respect your decision to stay with your boy
toy. Sometimes I get carried away.**

Is that an apology?

Will it matter if it is?

I won't hate you as much.

Yeah, it's an apology.

Forgiven. Now don't text me anymore.

I know, I know, you have a boyfriend.

I put my phone on silent and sat on the edge of my bed. Dirk
was refusing to take the hint, yet I was still allowing him to engage
me. Why did I text him back? I could have told him to get lost, but I
didn't. And I didn't know why.

Michael was friendly with other girls, but he didn't flirt with
them. He was polite and kind to everyone—it was that simple.
I knew how he felt about me too, even if things had been crazy
stressful for both of us lately.

My phone vibrated. There was another text from Dirk.

Sleep well, Airel.

I didn't know if he was trying to be annoying or charming.

Ellie told me she went out with him last week—said it was part
of "establishing her cover". She even went to one of his shows. She
said he was really talented. "He sings with the voice of an angel,"

she said, "and I should know."

I told her she could have him.

If I'd learned anything from being pursued by another man, it was that I really loved Michael. Dirk only helped me to realize Michael and I belonged together. He was my soul mate, if there was such a thing. I deeply hoped there was because I didn't want to live in a world where there wasn't. I didn't want to live in the kind of world where there wasn't any room for hopeless romantics. If anything, Dirk was pushing me toward Michael. The extra pressure wasn't going to change anything. Not for me.

PART TEN
THE SUCCESSION

CHAPTER I

Washington, D.C.—Present Day

ELLIE WORE DARK, OVERSIZED sunglasses and a hooded coat to hide her blue hair. She was a little pissed off that John had forced her to go all the way to D.C. instead of somewhere cool. But this was the price of the truth, and she would have the truth.

John walked toward a table for two, low light, back of the house. Ellie faded into nothing and moved in close enough to ensure she wouldn't miss anything. The longer she stayed invisible, the harder it was to get back together, and the more it hurt. Nothing was free, not even her gift.

A man at the table who appeared to be FBI, CIA or just a run-of-the-mill spook motioned for John to sit. He sat and both men sized one another up, then John ordered an espresso.

He seemed to relax a little after that. Ellie wondered how many meetings like this he'd had in his lifetime. "What do I call you?" he asked, his voice low.

"My op handle is PILLBOX, if you must call me anything other than 'sir'."

John swallowed. "Got it."

"I'll get down to business, John, because I know if I were in your position, I'd appreciate the courtesy. I'm working for an individual who will go by the name MAGICIAN, at least for now. This individual requires that you procure an item for them."

"I gather there's no brochure?"

"Don't get smart. It's real simple. You can either bring the item in, or we can turn the dogs loose on you and your family. You racked up quite a bit of debt over there in Cape Town when you decided to cowboy up."

John clenched his fists under the table, but his voice was steady. "I could have handled things differently, you know,"

"Yeah, you could have, John. But it wasn't working out in your favor. Besides, where would it have landed you?"

John sighed. "Tell me what you want."

"MAGICIAN wants you to bring back a little trinket. It's a precious stone. Looks like a ruby. We tracked it from South Africa to Zurich, where it changed hands. One of our guys tells us that its new handler took it on to the UK, that it's in or around Glasgow now."

"And where do I come in?"

PILLBOX dug around in his overcoat and produced an itinerary, sliding it forward on the table. "You fly out tomorrow morning."

John looked at the travel documents and pulled out boarding passes for a series of flights that went from Dulles to JFK to Heathrow to Edinburgh. He was already checked all the way through. The name on the tickets was Morgan Hale, U.S. diplomat, so customs wouldn't be an issue.

Ellie was impressed—these guys didn't mess around.

PILLBOX answered John's questioning glance by producing a folio that contained several thousand British pound notes in small denominations, and a passport that matched the tickets. "Don't worry. You look like a Hale, comma, Morgan. Hire a car in Edinburgh and drive. It's only about forty miles."

"Who's the mark?" John asked.

Ellie wondered if the mission was an assassination. *John's not into that kind of work, is he?*

PILLBOX tapped the folio, prompting John to shuffle through the papers. At the back was a thin dossier with the photo of a woman. As he stared at the black-and-white image, he asked, "Rules of engagement?"

"Improvise. Zero collateral—if possible. The mark keeps the item on her person at all times. Retrieve it however you can and return stateside. Hitch a ride with the waiting U.S. Air Force bird at RAF Lakenheath. They're expecting one VIP Morgan Hale within the next 24-48 hours. That C-37 will be standing by, and you can drive right onto the ramp with these credentials. The usual drill, really, John. Morgan. Further questions?"

"So I've become a jewel thief now?"

PILLBOX shrugged. "If you want to look at it like that. Really, what you are is a kept man. After you become a jewel thief, you can stop being both of those. Just as long as MAGICIAN gets what he/she wants."

"What's the attraction?"

Ellie knew the Bloodstone when she saw it. Now she was sure John was somehow involved in at least some of what had been going on with Airel. *Maybe not intentionally, but he's far deeper than she knows. I wonder if he's for us or against us.* Her thoughts turned dark as she wondered about the implications. *If John's connected with the Brotherhood...*

"I'll say it like this, John," PILLBOX said. "You have lots of experience running guns. We thought you'd be perfect for this job."

"So it's a weapon of some kind?"

"I never said any such thing." PILLBOX tapped his wristwatch. "Better get to work, John. That Air Force return ticket's only good for another couple of days." He stood and adjusted his overcoat. "Best of luck. And don't do anything I wouldn't do."

John sat at the table and watched the man walk out the front door into the December cold.

He said nothing. He sat and stared, looking lost.

Ellie wondered what he was thinking and decided to risk it. If she was the only immortal within range, tapping into his thoughts wouldn't give too much away. The implications of this meeting had too many possibilities. It was worth the risk. She concentrated and listened.

"How did I get here?" John thought. *"Didn't I used to be something more than a freakin' cog in the machine?"* John's thoughts came at Ellie in flashes of images—glimpses of royalty and majesty from some other time and place. The words PILLBOX and MAGICIAN rolled over and over the landscape of memories in his head, and Ellie could hear them echo back to her. John thought, *"It's time I get out of this business, focus on my family. Once this debt is paid, I'm out."*

He looked at the dossier again. *Eve Crawford. What do I need to know about you, Eve? Will I be forced to kill you? Will I be able to? And what about that stone? Tell me, Eve,* he thought, *why is that little trinket so very important to everybody?*

CHAPTER II

Boise, Idaho—Present Day

"YOU EXCITED FOR CHRISTMAS?" Ellie was being annoying—her cheerful nature made me want to choke her sometimes. "Tomorrow is the big day. Have I told you how much I love it?"

"Yeah," I said, mustering boatloads of sarcasm. "Is it ever going to be great! Dad's off doing whatever he does that's more important than his family, Michael and I finally make it to our first Christmas together and we don't even get to see each other, and Kreios is gone, dead, who knows. And my mom is being an overprotective sadist."

"Wow, Miss Bucket Full of Sunshine." Ellie lay on the couch, playing with her phone.

"Well, why should I be happy?" I was sitting in Dad's overstuffed chair with my laptop, researching climbing gear. Dirk was practically stalking me now. He was not only in Mr. Dorsey's math class, but he also got lumped in with me in a junior elective course for physical fitness. We both hated it, so that was one thing we had in common. It was some stupid new presidential initiative for fighting youth obesity or something, which meant we had to earn more credits doing something active. There weren't many options that were attractive to me, so I chose the one I thought would at least be a little fun—winter sports. In this case, the class had a heavy emphasis on climbing, and it was fun because we got to go to a climbing gym to learn the fundamentals, like being on belay and rappelling.

Naturally, Dirk chose climbing too. Big surprise.

"What," Ellie said, interrupting my parade of vitriol and sadness. "Are you telling me you have absolutely *nothing* to be happy about?"

"You tell me," I shot back. "Mom and Dad have grounded me for life. They stopped short of telling me that I should break up with Michael. And to top it all off, he's been moody and depressing to be around."

"Yeah, I can see how that could suck, being around someone who's all depressing and moody."

I cursed under my breath. "Fine, make jokes at my expense. Mom is the High Priestess of Discipline. I think she forgot what it was like to be our age—er, I mean *my* age." I felt so disrespected sometimes, like they didn't get it, or worse, like they *did* get it but didn't care. I was pretty sure my mom felt one of two ways—either she didn't know how much Michael's emotional support meant to me, or she knew exactly how much it meant to me, which was why she was trying to keep us apart. Didn't she know she couldn't stop me from growing up? I felt like she thought I was breakable, that I would shatter in stiff wind.

"You did break your curfew," Ellie said in a whisper.

"Hey, whose side are you on, anyway?"

"I'm on my side, which is the right side, mind you. But we're not talking about me. Tell me what's up with your dad—missing

Christmas is lame, especially with all the stuff that's been going on."

"Tell me about it. He's been gone a lot. Especially lately. It's like he's on some secret mission for the government or something." All I wanted was to move out early. Maybe then I would find out if my parents cared enough to notice if I was gone.

Ellie cocked an eyebrow at me. "The government? Do tell. Your dad work for the CIA or something?"

"Who cares? For all I know, he could be James freakin' Bond."

"He's certainly bold enough, tailing your sorry butt halfway across the world. Anyway, my bet is he's not a vacuum cleaner salesman." She laughed and eyed me when I didn't join her. "Oh. I see you're going to keep this sunshiny mood going. Fun."

"It's lots of fun to be grounded," I said.

"Well, you knew the consequences, right? And you blew right through 'em."

"Still, though."

"Still what? Your mum and dad are a little freaked out about you, and justifiably so, considering all that's happened. They told you what they expected from you. You disobeyed. Punishment is how you learn."

"Kindness leads to repentance," I countered.

She laughed loudly. "Yeah, but only if that kindness *means* something to the person on the receiving end. From what I can tell, you've been right pissed off at your parents for a couple of months now, ever since you got back. You've an axe to grind, my friend."

I glossed over the fact that she hadn't been back as long as I had. *Or had she?* "So?"

"I know 'furious vengeance' when I see it. That's all." She made air quotes.

I stewed. I said though my teeth very quietly, "Don't I have the right?"

"Psh. You're a child, mate. What do you know?"

I was shocked and allowed my jaw to fall onto the carpet. I probed my mind for *She,* but all I got was a sense that I was being mocked by the whole entire world. I felt stupid and undignified.

"I know what you're thinking," Ellie said, "even without trying to read your mind—'How dare you?' Am I right?"

I scowled. "I like you better when you act like a teenager; like my friend and not another parent. I already have two."

"I know you don't want any advice, but I'll give you some for free anyway. Calm yourself. Nobody owes you anything. When your life stops being all about you, adulthood can begin. But it won't until then. Try a little humility."

I stared at her for a full minute, trying to come up with one word to say to her. *Kreios is gone and now I get his daughter lecturing me. Yay, Airel.* Finally I said, "Let's talk about something else."

"Gladly," she said. "How about your little research project over there?" She pointed to my laptop. "Daydreaming about the climbing trip, are we?"

I wanted to ask her not to use such a condescending tone, but restrained myself. I knew I wouldn't get anywhere with her. "Actually, yeah." Our climbing guru, who told us to call him Shane, was a real laid-back expert who had been working with us at the gym. He was cool. He was going to take our class out to the cliffs along Highway 21 in a few weeks right outside of town and show us how it was done for real. So yes, I was daydreaming. It was the last exciting thing in my life at the moment. I wanted to tell Ellie it wasn't like there was anything else for me to do, but I was sure she would have more coals of red-hot wisdom to drop on my head if I tried.

"Well, I'm stoked about it, mate. I suppose I should have told you that I fully intend to crash your little field trip party."

I was not surprised to hear it, and though I tried to conceal my joy, I actually smiled. "Really?"

"Really, girlie. I figure senior skip day's in May, but I need an early reprieve. Besides, I hear Dirk will be there. I gotta keep him on the hook, if you know what I mean."

I rolled my eyes. "You're not even registered as a senior, Ellie, so never mind senior skip day, but you're planning on skipping in the middle of January? Why? Just cuz?"

She looked at me like it was obvious. "I like being around you. Even when you're grumps."

"Try again." But I smiled.

"I am bored out of my mind."

I groaned and threw a couch pillow at her. I stood up. "All right, weirdette. Hot chocolate or tea?"

"You know me. Earl Grey all the way."

I walked to the kitchen, and as I turned away from her, my eyes welled up. I was really glad I had her in my life. Even though she was exasperating, she was good for me. She was probably right about almost everything. She felt like family. And as I put the kettle on for her, I couldn't help wondering when—or if—I would ever see Kreios again.

CHAPTER III

Arabia—800 B.C.

URIEL WADDLED FROM THE fireside to the bed and eased herself down. Any day now, she would be a mother. There had been new pains in the womb that came and went in a quickening rhythm, faster and more intense and more often from day to day now. She knew it would be time for the birth soon.

She was filled to brimming with so many conflicting emotions about the baby that she wasn't sure what to think. She was excited and terrified. She felt the most profound peace she had ever felt in her entire life, and yet she had never felt more vulnerable, either.

She smiled as she stroked the roundness of her belly, cooing at her unborn child. "You will be a boy," she said.

She wished there was someone to answer her statement, that there was even someone to attempt to refute it, or someone to glow with it as she glowed.

But there was no one.

She thought back over the circumstances of her pregnancy, about how she had been daring and extravagant with a handsome young man just over nine months ago, how she had taken the

ultimate risk on him, and how those few hours of surrender
to feelings she had never before fully indulged had changed
everything. She thought about how the child's father, Yshmial, had
so obviously—when it was over—not shared those feelings with
her, at least not to the depth she had felt them. And indeed still felt
them, from time to time.

She had given him everything. And he had taken everything
she'd given and then left her, without remorse. He had at least
given her a son, she hoped. If it wasn't for her angelic abilities, he
would also have given her a life of extreme poverty and shame.
But hopefully she would be able to give her child whatever they
needed, including security. *I can take what we need, and if we are
threatened, I can vanish with him into the air and make our escape.*
All that would remain would be the shame. Only she—she alone—
would know of that and carry it.

That is an acceptable trade. I cannot change anything else.

She hadn't tried to exercise her abilities since she had first felt
the profound change come over her. She didn't dare harm this new
life by trying anything impossible, doing anything a human couldn't
do. It was too risky.

Memories of her inheritance haunted her. She wondered if she
was doomed to die in childbirth, as her mother had succumbed. Was
she cursed to follow in the exact same fashion? She didn't know.
And what of the child? Would he survive? How long would she be
able to keep him, to be his mother, until she risked activating in him
the same abilities that had been activated in her, thereby bringing
so much risk and worry to both of them? There were certainly no
guarantees now.

"He will be named Qiel," she said. "That is what I shall name
him." And now, as if in response to his name, the boy began to
move vigorously. Something burst within her and issued forth,

soaking her. The baby was coming now. There would be no turning back from the pain, the struggle, the anxiety.

There was no one to help here. *Here, where it has been safe now for these nine cycles of the moon...* In a shelter near a high woodline in the mountains, where she had been safe all this time, where she had been preparing, as the day drew near, as everything became full and ripe and mature—and changed in ways she had never foreseen.

She was all alone—*for now,* she thought. *Only for now. Soon there will be two of us.*

Now, for the first time in a very long time, she thought of her father, Kreios, and longed for him. She was starting to understand how he must feel, must have felt always, toward her. Being a parent would change everything.

CHAPTER IV

Sawtooth Mountains of Idaho—Present Day

ELLIE HADN'T THOUGHT IT was going to be so uncomfortable, bringing Airel back to her father's house. But it was. For both of them. She couldn't quite place her finger on why. Or perhaps *I'm not ready to admit to what I suspect.* "You all right, girlie?"

Airel looked at her with haunted eyes. "Sure."

Ellie chuckled. "You don't have to lie to make friends."

Airel wasn't amused. "I'm not making friends. I already have you." She looked around Kreios's library, up to the high crenellated stone walls and the coffered ceilings they supported. "This place has too much going on."

"What do you mean?"

Airel pointed to the blazing fireplace. "Did you light it? No. Neither of us did."

"And?"

Airel exhaled heavily. "I don't want to say."

Ellie walked to her side and touched her arm. "Hey. This is my dad's place. It's safe here. I promise. Okay?"

"Promises."

Ellie had to growl a little at that.

Airel turned around again, looking at the walls, the high wooden shelves holding volumes that were ten times older than she was, and scrolls, even. "There are ghosts here, Ellie. I feel them. The last time I was here, bad things happened, and Kim—"

Ellie could see that she was crying. She let her. She walked to a wingback chair near the fire and lounged on it, swinging a leg up over the arm and tucking her bright blue head into its deep corner. She listened to the crackle of the fire, burning wood for fuel, wood that was either never consumed or always miraculously replenished. *What would be the difference?*

Airel went on, speaking through her tears. "It's just that it's weird here now. Without them. Last time Michael was here, it was … different. And Kreios … do you know where he is?"

"Haven't a clue." Ellie nibbled a bit of dead skin from a fingertip and then spat it toward the fire. This dead skin thing had started happening again—in the past fifty or so years—and she figured she was starting to show her age now. In another couple hundred years, she might be aged enough in her appearance to be able to legally buy alcohol. Unless social mores changed by then. She had been given wine as a child quite often, though it was usually mixed with water. She snapped out of her reverie. "I imagine, though, that when he wants to show up, he'll show up."

Airel breathed, sitting down on the loveseat that faced the fire. She kicked off her boots and tucked her feet up under her and then changed the subject. "I wish I had coffee."

"You and me both. Or a cup of Earl Grey."

Airel grunted and fiddled with the seam of her jeans. "Thanks for breaking me out of my high tower, by the way. What on earth did you say to my mom that got her to agree to this little trip?"

"Oh, nothing. Just that 'the world's gone mad,' and, 'kids

these days,' and then I nodded sympathetically with a couple of her assessments and told her I needed some time in Sun Valley with my bestie."

"Really. That was all it took? And you bought us three days?"

"Yeah. She seemed impressed with me. Well ... and my car." She was referring to her brand-new bright blue Toyota FJ 4x4. Ellie had told her when she first showed it off that she'd bought it because it went with her hair. "I guess she thought it was big and buff enough to be quote-unquote safe, and that it was part of the reason she figured you would be in good hands."

"Whatever." Airel crossed her arms.

"And," Ellie continued, "I was pretty convincing, if I say so myself. I don't know why Americans get all googly-eyed over a person who speaks the English language properly. But they do." She dismissed the idea with the wave of her hand.

"Well, thanks. I needed to get out."

"Yeah, you did. I wanted to get up here too. We both need to spend some time outside the bounds."

"I know what you mean."

Ellie cleared her throat. "Actually, you might only know a little bit. You may not know what you think you know."

I WAS A LITTLE BLOWN away by Ellie still, even now. It was like being friends and hanging out with a rock star. Anything could happen. And it often did. "So," I said, "what is it that I think I know?"

"I want to start off by telling you a little more of my story," she said. I'd heard bits and pieces of her history over the time we'd known each other, but in true Ellie-style, she reserved all the juicy bits until the moment came along, inevitably, when she could shock me the most.

"Bring it on," I said.

"As far as being outside the bounds…" She appeared to reconsider for a moment. "Let's cover that in a minute. I wanna tell you a story first. Game?"

"Sure," I said, wondering what I was getting myself into. I fluffed a couch pillow and gave her my "I'm ready" signal, and then she plunged ahead.

"It's obvious I'm a mother, right? I mean, how else could the line have carried on if I wasn't."

"What?" I felt so stupid. *Of course.* And yet I made myself look stupider by shrieking my disbelief.

"Yeah, girlie. It's hitting you, isn't it?" She grinned. She allowed me a moment to let everything sink in, and then she carried on. "I've gotta say, I admire your commitment to sexual integrity with Michael. I know how difficult it is sometimes, especially when there are intense feelings involved."

"Yeah, well … it's not all roses with Michael," I said, trying to voice my growing inner concern about the fact that something in regard to Michael was eating away at me. It was mostly formless and void, though, and now wasn't the time to discuss it anyway.

"Oh. Well, it'll get better in time. Right?"

"Right," I said, barely able to believe myself.

"Well, in my case," Ellie said, graciously moving on, "those intense feelings weren't reciprocated beneath the surface, and I deceived myself. Or I allowed myself to be deceived, whatever the case. In the end, I turned up preggers."

Echoes of Kim. More emotion. I nodded and blinked away the rapidly increasing moisture in my eyes.

"The father—his name was Yshmial, but that doesn't really

matter. What really matters is his lineage, which I'll get to eventually. I went into hiding when I knew I was carrying a child. I knew right away, and I abstained from my gift entirely while I was pregnant. I didn't want any harm to come to him."

"It was a boy? You knew?"

"Yeah. I knew it. I found a quiet place for us. Made a nest for us in the deep wilderness, in a high meadow near the edge of a wood. I built us a shelter from fallen branches and pine boughs, covering it with the skins of animals I harvested as I waited to come to term. I gave birth to Qiel alone, without any help from anyone." There shone in her eyes a defiant pride mixed with heavy grief.

"And he was okay?"

"Yeah. He was beautiful." She smiled, radiant.

"What happened then?"

She paused, and my question snapped her out of something. "He grew up too fast." She stopped again, and it seemed like she was done talking about it.

"Okay…"

"Come on," she said, standing. "I want to show you something outside the bounds."

I stood and followed her out of the library and down the hall, the curving one with the torches hanging near the double doors that led into Kreios's bedroom. This was the place I had come when I was playing ninja girl, trying to gather intel so I could escape from a psychopathic killer/kidnapper. "So what is it, Ellie? Are you planning on us playing dress up together or something?" I alluded to the closet where I had seen Kreios's treasure trove of costumes, period fashions from every era.

"Not this time, but maybe someday when we both feel like being three-year-olds, we can." She smiled wickedly at me. "I want to show you the Threshold."

"The Threshold? What's that?"

"You'll have to see it to believe it."

I laughed, thinking of the word and its meaning. "Should I have brought my boots?" I looked down at the socks on my feet.

Ellie walked to a steel door, resting one hand on its doorknob, and then turned and looked at me. "Actually, yeah. Maybe you should have, at least if we were to walk through this door." She closed her eyes and turned back toward it, concentrating.

This was the room I had found that night, the one that was a little cubicle of concrete and nothing else. Before I could form an opinion on all this, she threw open the door.

"What the—"

"Pick up your jaw from the floor, mate. It is real."

"That can't be real," I said, my mouth a little numb.

"Behold," she said grandiosely, "the city of Glasgow."

It was true. We were looking out from a high hill over an entire city at dusk, the view framed by the closet door, which itself was now evidently in the midst of a Victorian cemetery. A great stone angel monument stood in the foreground, what looked like a tomb marker, and farther on and below stood cathedral spires, the buildings of a modern civilization.

"This is," Ellie said, "one of the thin places." She touched my arm and I glanced back toward her. "It's the reason Kreios built his house here."

CHAPTER V

Glasgow, Scotland—Present Day

ELLIE FOUND JOHN RIGHT before he boarded the charter C-37. She missed him in Glasgow, but planned to listen to his thoughts on the ride back to the U.S. and find out what happened to the woman he was hunting and if he found the Bloodstone.

John looked out the small window as the English countryside slid by under the wings, giving way to the icy waters of the North Atlantic. *"I'm going home. It feels so good, really, to fail at this kind of stuff."*

Nothing had gone according to plan for John Cross. He hadn't been able to find much at all on one Eve Crawford back in D.C. using the Web, so he figured he could get something locally once he was on site in Scotland. Maybe talk to some shopkeepers and landlords, work the streets for better information. *"That proved to be a rather ill-advised roll of the dice. I didn't think I was gambling on that score, but apparently I was."*

Ellie let him think. She found a seat in the back where she could close her eyes and try to get a little rest.

"Eve Crawford was a shell identity. But why go to all that

trouble?"

John kept trying, unsuccessfully, to block out of his mind the idea that he or his family might have to pay a serious price for all this. He imagined the displeasure this turn of events would produce in PILLBOX, let alone MAGICIAN, whoever that was.

She could tell he was glad not to have another murder on his hands. But he was sad he had missed Christmas with his family. Again. *"I told myself this wasn't going to keep on happening, especially after what went down in Kigali. And in Potosi. Rwanda. Bolivia. Hostile situations. I got out with barely more than my own skin intact. It's a tough business, dealing in force with backstreet thugs, and I swore more than once I'd had enough of it. The only times I sleep well are in my own bed, by the side of my own wife, my arms around the one woman I love."*

As the C-37 reeled off the miles beneath, John briefly allowed his mind to go, to haunt the depths of depravity and think on what might happen if worse came to worst. What would MAGICIAN do to him now that he'd failed?

Would there be a second chance?

CHAPTER VI

Sawtooth Mountains of Idaho—Present Day

WE WERE SEATED BACK in the library before my world really started to fall apart again. Why is my whole life under attack?

I felt *She* rustling in the back of my mind once more, felt like I was standing on the edge of something enormous in my life, like I was about to do or hear or learn something that would change everything yet again. It was both exhausting and exhilarating. *"Hold on tight,"* She said, *"and remember who you are."*

"Amazing, isn't it?" Ellie asked me, referring to what we had just seen in the closet.

"'Amazing' doesn't quite cut it," I said, "when you have a whole city in your closet. So what are you telling me? That the little concrete room—what did you call it?"

"The Threshold."

"Yeah, that. You're telling me that when I open that door, I can walk straight through to a graveyard in Scotland?"

"Yeah. And lots of other places."

"What? How is that even possible?"

"See, there are these thin places in the world. This is one of the very first. It's how Kreios was able to find his Book. As the world under the sun has aged, there have been, through natural decay, lots of other thin places popping up. Did you ever read *The Lord of the Rings?*"

"Of course. I'm a fantasy nerd *par excellence.*"

"Then you remember the Palantir. The seeing stones?"

"Oh, yeah. It's part of what corrupted the world of men and linked Eisengard to Mordor."

Ellie looked impressed with that, like it wasn't where she was trying to steer me, like it was an unanticipated wrinkle. "True. The way the Threshold works is similar, but different. Wherever there's another thin place, if you're concentrating hard enough on where you'd like to go or what you'd like to find, the Threshold takes you there. At least, as long as you're either an angel or a half-breed, like us."

"How does *that* work?"

"The thin places are where the natural realm has worn away over time, where the eternal, the everlasting, is beginning to break through. If you didn't know any better, you'd say those places are haunted, even demonic. And in some cases, depending on the circumstance, you might be right. But all it really means is that the world under the sun is wearing out. Quite literally."

"And because of this 'Threshold,' as you call it, we can what, go places instantly? Like teleportation?"

"Nope. It's not like that."

I felt something familiar begin to ruffle within me. I wasn't sure what it was. I hadn't felt it in a long time. It was a sweet pain, a longing. "Then what is it like?"

"Airel, the eternal—the spiritual—is what this world was created *out of.* The 'natural', as we know it, including time itself, is passing away. The everlasting is beginning to punch through, assert itself over what amounts to an unclean usurper, an illusion in the final analysis."

"The natural world—under the sun—you mean everything we can see is an illusion?"

"From El's—from an angelic perspective, yes. It's passing away, Airel. And when anyone crosses over the Threshold, they're crossing not just from place to place under the sun. They're crossing out of time as well."

I wrinkled my brows in consternation, widening my eyes. "Time travel?"

Ellie shook her head slowly. "It all depends. And one must be careful in there." She pointed down that long hallway, at the end of which loomed what I was thinking of more and more as a doomsday device of some kind. "It's best to close your eyes. It's not called the Threshold for nothing."

"So when I go—if I *ever* go—in there, exactly what is it I'll be on the threshold *of?*"

Before she could answer, I was overcome by that feeling again, that familiar sense that I couldn't quite place, and I nearly collapsed on the floor. I caught myself, tried to breathe, and rubbed my head with my fingers.

"You feel it too, don't you?" Ellie asked.

"What is it?"

"Kreios. He's coming." She looked very sad, especially in light of this new information.

I thought she should be ecstatic.

"Ellie," I said, trying to think how I wanted to phrase my question, "what is it you're not telling me?" As far as I was concerned, I was extremely excited to see Kreios, and I didn't get why she'd be *sad,* of all things.

She stood and walked to the mantel, the shelf above the

fireplace. This was where the Books were kept—the Book of Kreios, my Book, other books and odds and ends I wasn't sure of. I hadn't thought much of it until that moment, but then it suddenly hit me—*Where's mine?* I didn't know. *I could have sworn it was up there with the rest of them, but it's gone.*

Ellie took down a familiar volume and handed it to me.

In confirmation of my internal question, the name resounded within my being, ringing like a house-sized bell. KREIOS. I opened the cover.

"Read," she said.

I looked up at her, questions in my eyes. *Why? And where's mine? And where's your Book, Ellie?*

"But before you start, you need to know something about me."

I groaned. "What is it now? How come you like to play these mind games? I hate this."

She snorted. "I'm not playing games, Airel. I'm trying to protect you. I wasn't lying when I said that before, on Wideawake Airfield. I am here to protect you. But as you read this," she gestured to the Book of Kreios, "you're going to find out why. And when you do, you're going to be angry enough about it to want to kill me."

I was shocked. All I could say was, "What?"

"Kreios will be here soon. Read up. I'm going to the kitchen for a nosh. Bring you a coffee?"

I flashed her an *"are you freaking crazy"* look and shook my head, wondering what on earth she was talking about, and also what *exactly* she told my mom in order to get her to allow me to come up here. "I will never want to kill you, Ellie, no matter what. You are my blood, my friend."

"Thanks, Airel, but never say never."

I reached out to *She. Do I really know Ellie at all?* I got this feeling that meant I already knew the answer. I hated that feeling. So much.

Ellie half turned to go, and then stopped. "You read your Bible, yeah?"

"Of course." That wasn't true—I was no scholar of biblical studies. I didn't want to look bad.

"You know who Judas Iscariot was, then."

My stomach felt like there was lodged within it a fist of ice. "Doesn't everyone?"

"Yeah, well. In life's play, that was my primary role. The traitor." She turned and walked away.

Stunned, I walked back to the library, curled up on the couch, and then opened the Book of Kreios.

The Book let me in this time, took me further than I'd been before, let me see pieces of the story it had withheld from me until now. I read about loss and hurt and traitorous pacts made with wicked men, about Uriel's activation, about her ability, about the legend of the Derakhshan. And still more.

About her son.

CHAPTER VII

Arabia—788 B.C.

QIEL HAD JUST TURNED twelve. It wasn't two months ago, and his mother wondered many things about how to proceed as his only parent. How can I teach him to be a man? She looked around at the little shop she had managed to build for them in one of the towns of men. These little trinkets she crafted and sold—inkwells and pens, paper, the tools of the scribe; brushes, reeds, inkstones, paperweights—these were all so meager, and the life they now lived together was nothing if not humble.

It was, she realized, a perfect opposite to everything she lived for before Qiel had come along. He had changed everything—everything that was possible to be changed.

Should I now abandon him to another? Someone, a man, who would show him how to embrace true masculinity? Someone not part of the Brotherhood? Someone who will not, no matter what he intends, she thought bitterly, *activate his gift? Someone who will not, no matter what he intends, shine it like a beacon in pure darkness, beckoning the Horde to come and kill him?*

Uriel's life was drifting in uncharted waters—all of it. While

she knew this, and while she had made her peace with it as much
as she could, she still wondered in these moments why El had
consigned her to such an existence. She had ceased to ask the
question aloud many years ago.

She stood at a crossroads in every sense, and neither path
looked suitable or even reasonable. If she were to keep Qiel close,
try to keep him safe, he would turn—if he hadn't already—and
when he did, what might his reaction be? He would hate her,
probably as much as she had hated her own father. *But not now. Oh,
to have certain decisions to make over again.* The cup of their lives
would be filled to brimming with misunderstanding and hatred and
ultimatum. Already the boy knew there was something different
about their lives. *Indeed, how could he miss it?*

But what if she were to let him go now? He would not
understand. He would feel abandoned. Rejected. He would not
understand that it would be for his own safety, that her decision to
leave him, to send him out into the world at this young age, was
for his own good, his safekeeping. But what would he do? Where
would he go, and to whom would he cling for shelter, for love and
for peace, for food and clothing? Would he come into manhood in
the filth of the gutters, surviving on what morsel he might beg from
those in the streets more respectable than he? *Than we?*

Had she raised a beggar? Had they come all this way for
nothing? Would there be no end to consequence in her life, in the
lives of those she loved?

"Mama," Qiel called to her, ducking in from the blinding sun
outside under the blanket draped at the entrance to their little shop.

"I'm here," she said, standing from where she had been
kneeling behind one of the tables that held her wares.

"Oh, there you are," he said. He was already taller than she was,
though that wasn't saying much. Some in the village mistook her for

a child, at least at first. "What's wrong, Mama?"

"Nothing."

"You had a funny look on your face."

"No, I didn't."

Qiel screwed up his own face as he regarded her.

Her heart thundered with fell anticipation; something terrible was going to happen soon if she didn't do something. *But what? What decision should she make? How could a mother choose between two different kinds of damnation for her son? Was there no alternative?*

"You cannot fool me, Mama."

She gasped in playful shock.

He smiled. "Mama, there is a rich man in the square hoping to buy a paperweight for his scribe. I told him to come, but he was very specific about the kind of weight he desired."

"Good. Let him come," Uriel said, crouching down again to the small crate she had been unloading. She took two such stones from it and laid them on the table before her. "We have what he requires. Even if he does not yet know it." She winked at her son.

"Yes, but he said he wants a red one, and we don't have—" Qiel was interrupted by the blinding light of the rug flap being drawn aside at the entrance. In came a tall, cloaked man, his hood drawn low over his white-bearded face. "Oh, sir. You're here. We were getting our paperweights ready to present to you."

The man did not look up or reveal his face but strode quickly into the shop, hands tucked away out of sight.

Uriel noticed this, but didn't put up her guard like she would have in the past—when she was a warrior, not a mother.

Before she could react, before she gave the first thought to the powers of her gift, now long dormant and unexercised, it came. From out of the folds of the man's robe a thin reed rose up against

her, and with a small blast of air, the poison barb launched and
sailed, pricking her throat and fouling her angelic blood with its
payload.

As her vision began to fade, her ears rang with the whine of
the drug's effects, and she heard the screams of her son as the man
in the cloak seized him bodily. *Oh, El. There is a third way. Qiel...*
She faded from the world, wishing she could weep but lacking the
strength or the will. She saw Anael turn and leave with her son in
his arms.

WHEN URIEL AWOKE, SHE was no longer in the village. She
was in a dark, cool place, her breath a vapor, the air a fume of dank
fungus that racked her lungs and assailed each breath she took,
making her wheeze and cough.

The first thing she thought was, *Where is my son?* The first
feeling with which her heart was seized was terror, and not for
herself, but for Qiel.

She opened her eyes. She struggled to focus—everything was
hazed and milky white.

She heard a voice.

"Before you begin to get too creative with your gift, Uriel, you
must know first that I hold all power over you now."

Anael. Traitors could never rest easy in the company of thieves.
Uriel knew already that her worst fears had come upon her, had
overtaken her. *Anael has my son; he will use Qiel as his token for
trade.* A dark titter of laughter swept over her, and she smelled
Anael's rot. He was close.

"You have already guessed my game—good. I smell
despondency upon you. Let us not waste any words. You will bring

me the stone—surely you remember what pact we crafted between us over four hundred years ago?"

She managed a groan as she tried to come to herself, but it was mostly in vain, like puffing air into a great canvas sack in an attempt to fill it round. She reached for the limits of her body—as she would do when remanifesting from having dispersed herself into the air—but those limits were vague and unreachable. Yet she felt her body was sound. Only numbness. *What was on the tip of the barb with which he poisoned me?* She filled with alarm.

Anael continued. "When I possess the stone, I shall return your son to you, greasy traitoress. He shall be as you have known him to be, but oh," he snorted, "apart from one difference." He leaned closer, and she began to suffer from his rank breath. "I am afraid the boy has started to metamorphose. Regrettable," he said, his tone nonchalant. "I do not suppose I can pretend to know how many more days will be allotted to him, even if you were to fulfill our covenant and earn his release. Many Brothers will pursue the spark his life emits under the sun and seek to snuff it." He backed away from her prone and motionless body. "But such things," a wicked smile became audible in his tone, "tend to make one's life … compelling. Yes. The compulsion will drive you as you were meant to be driven—like a dumb beast." He struck her.

She could hear the footsteps he made as he took his leave of her.

"I shall return with instructions when you are lucid. If you betray me again, your son will die."

She fell again into darkness.

CHAPTER VIII

Mountains of Hijaz—Present Day

THE HOST WERE VERY old. They were among the first of the angelic creatures created, and they swore fealty to the Maker of all things. El gave them orders and they carried them out with all their being.

They were the guards of old, from legend and myth. Hidden beyond the sight and reach of man, Eden grew more lush and beautiful than on the day it was created. The Host did not only guard the entrance, they also tended the garden and lived on the sands of its shores and among the fronds of its jungles.

Only once had anyone dared challenge the gates of Eden. This one was spared his life, but only because El himself held their swords.

For thousands of years, they lived in peace, made strong by constant training and wise by council with El. They made their homes in a small city near the gate of Eden and prepared for the war that never came. Some of the Host grew tired of the stories, of the threat that never materialized. They were the Host of the Most High—lethal, and created to wage war. Why did they train, and why had they been made, if war would never come? The waiting was harder than the Host imagined any war might be, but things as of late were changing.

"Do you feel it, the darkness?" Some called him 'lord', as he was the head, but in all things, the Host thought as one. Separate names and identities were of no use.

"Yes, my lord. It is as if the world beyond is dying. The gate is as strong as ever, but I feel the ground it stands upon is growing weak."

Both stood atop the city wall overlooking the garden, the city at their backs and the darkness beyond.

"The Tree of Life must be protected at any cost. The time of our created purpose is at hand, though this, I fear, is not the war we once thought we would fight. Something more evil is coming. Something we may not be able to overcome."

Glasgow, Scotland—Present Day

JORDAN WESTON STOOD ALONE in a cluster of trees at the south edge of the Necropolis in Glasgow, looking over the monuments to the dead toward the gothic Glasgow Cathedral's corroded green roof.

He was trying to concentrate, but the pain in his un-good hand, the pestilent pattering of the rain—these were distracting him. This mausoleum, which was the final resting place for the bones of one Major Archibald Monteath, was only one of many convenient access points to the spirit realm. A thin place. *Most of the British Isles are thin now,* he thought. *Once an empire upon which the sun never set.* "Until, of course, it did." He didn't laugh at his joke because he never laughed. And he didn't joke.

He strode forward under drooping skies of clay toward the pedimented door of the tomb. Through this thin place were the walls, the very gate to Eden. Beyond that stood the Tree of Life. The Tree had never been taken by the Brotherhood.

The door to this place had only been used once, only by Jordan, and long ago. He held his un-good hand and rubbed the tips of his dead fingers. *There is a cost. There is always a cost.*

Jordan turned and took stock of his army. Ten thousand regulars of the Brotherhood horde, half of it humans, half demons—and all gathered for him. He wasn't Seer, but he knew how wars were won. "Brothers." His voice boomed over the men and beasts before him. "Today will mark the beginning of a new world, a world where we rule from the shadows cast by the light of a red sun."

His army cheered and roared as demons sounded their approval.

"Now bond with your Brothers and take back what is yours." Wings flapped and tails whipped as the men and demons merged into five thousand. Their commander remained and bowed before Jordan.

"Take them through, find out how many there are, and report back to me," Jordan said. "Do not attack until I give the command. There are a few things yet to be accomplished on this end before we have the full advantage."

"Yes, lord. I will not fail you." The commander was the last of the Uri. He was unlike most of his dead brothers, as he was not a huge dragon. His pure-white skin was beautiful, with smooth scales and wings like silk. But he was as deadly as any Uri. He was perfect for this job, as he had unfinished business with the Sons of El.

"I know you will not fail, Commander. Now make ready. You will not have much time when the door is opened."

Jordan turned and found the opening for the key near the door. Without any hesitation, he thrust his un-good hand into the opening.

Pain seized him. The door groaned and split in half from bottom to top, yawning open wide.

Screams and the cries of trapped souls tore at the night sky. The white Uri commander ordered the horde army through. With a battle cry, they ran two by two into the darkness.

Jordan kept his hand steady in the keyhole, but his legs shook. The hand that felt nothing now felt everything. Blood, bone and nerves all came alive as what felt like hot coals melted into his skin. He held as long as he could, but when the white tail of the commander slipped into the darkness, he yanked his hand free. He fell to the ground, wailing.

The door sealed again quickly, dust billowed up around him, and the screams of the damned cut off. There was silence all around. A deep-rooted throbbing overtook his hand and now his arm almost to the shoulder. Now his un-good hand was his un-good arm.

He cursed. It was numb, yet it ached constantly. How could such a thing be?

Some thought him to be human, but he was not, strictly speaking. *Appearances are deceiving.* His given name was Jikininki, but the strategic necessity for the Brotherhood to stand near such a powerful collection of thin places under the sun as was represented here in Glasgow precipitated a geographic move from his old haunts, plus a change of disguise. The mask of humanity he now wore looked, smelled, moved, and talked like a Glaswegian. Like Jordan Weston.

Beneath, though, Jiki was as powerful a Rakshasa half-demonic prince as there ever was. Further, he knew that his humanity was not in fact a liability. He knew it actually made him much stronger, like the halfbreeds who served the enemy.

Jiki was a corpse-eater. He preferred them fresh lately, though—maybe it was all the chemicals they pumped into bodies these days. His arm would feel better after he ate, perhaps. Tonight he might make his own corpse, and nothing was as appealing as a warm one. Today he deserved a reward.

Perhaps soon he would see with his own eyes the battlefields he truly desired, those ripening for conquest. With the new Seer at his side—the true heir, not this Alexander pretender—Jiki would become preeminent.

VALAC MANIFESTED ON THE sidewalks of Zurich as a small street boy, walking its gutters in dirty old torn clothes. Who was Emerald Ruby? He scoffed. "Nobody." A name to use, an identity to assume, but now that vessel had outlived its usefulness for the shapeshifter and she was discarded. Emerald Ruby had gone the way of all things. Valac doubted he would need to take that form again.

As for the book seller, that pudgy worm from South Africa, he had been a tasty snack, especially the innards. In the end, men like Frank Wiseman were easy to deceive because they were all too willing. They liked to have their ears tickled. *It's all there in the Book. Enough of it, anyway.*

Valac the assassin, with thirty-eight legions of Brothers under his command, had cast off his feminine mask of deception and taken on his true form: that of an innocent little boy. And Valac was making good time—he would make it across town to fetch his pet before the sun rose.

Though he now possessed the Bloodstone and the Book of Airel, he considered doing yet one more little thing. *What to do about Airel? Should she live or die?* It would not be something to sweat too hard over, but it would take some talent to get to her, for she could keep herself from being drained by his kind. He knew she possessed the Sword of Light, which had slain many of his Brothers. He was no fool. No. He would wait before he used the gift he was famous for, the reason he was the most feared assassin among the Brotherhood. *It's best to report first and get paid for these trinkets. Then I can consider...extracurriculars.* He chuckled.

Something of a plan began to emerge in his mind. There were rumors of the Other, the rightful bloodline heir to the Bloodstone, the true Seer. Jiki was looking for him ... *Maybe the girl Airel can be used as bait, or even the Bloodstone.* Most believed the Alexander was the rightful heir, but if played right, the two sides could be fixed in conflict against each other. This was a thing he would ponder more upon.

He turned down a causeway by the lake, heading toward a warehouse building. *My pet,* he called in his mind, *it is time to come out and play.*

Ahead, a large door on the jetty rolled aside in the darkness, and slithering out like a snake, sliding like a river of excrement from the opening, came his pet. In the darkness of predawn night, it uncoiled itself and stood, unfurling terrible wings that spanned a thousand meters across, its two heads snorting and smoking black fumes from each set of nostrils. Valac continued walking, coming closer to the beast, calling to it in his mind.

The beast knelt so he could mount it, and then with a powerful sweep of the wings, it launched Valac on its back into the night sky.

CHAPTER IX

Sawtooth Mountains of Idaho—Present Day

ELLIE HADN'T REALLY BEEN hungry at all; she had no appetite lately. She had only come to the kitchen to escape. She didn't know what else to do, where else to go—she couldn't be in the room while Airel read the story of her heartless betrayal, her utter failure as a descendant of Kreios.

Plus there was another pain. Familiar, yes, but far younger.

She rubbed her sternum, where the swirling birthmarks that had identified her as a descendant of the angel Kreios once glowed silver-blue. Now they were mostly obscured, though at first she had thought nothing of it. It was a mysterious bruise that had appeared days ago. She'd noticed it in the mirror at the center of her chest after her evening shower.

As time went on, it became obvious—it was the Mark of the Bloodstone. It had never been completely removed from her. No matter what she did to try to remove it—whether in using her power of transportation by molecular disintegration or by appealing to El—it remained.

It was a part of her now.

She tried to think rationally, but it was difficult for her not to imagine her own death, and indeed that the second death, too—the eternal punishment—might be lurking for her in shadows, waiting to take her. She wondered how the Mark clung to her.

She rubbed at the wound as it slowly spread over her heart.

I must have bonded with the Bloodstone at Mard Castle all those centuries ago. That must be how it clings to me now. I was so foolish to think . . . She shook her head, remembering what had happened then.

And then a new thought came. *If the Mark hasn't fully passed from me, was I able to make it fully pass from Michael? Or did I fail—have I merely spread the disease?*

Ellie locked her hands behind her neck and tilted her head back, closing her eyes, breathing. "No matter what I try to do to make it right," she whispered to herself, a tear forming in her eye, "I cannot succeed." She breathed deeper, trying to control herself. *Have I not paid my penance, El? Have I not yet endured enough pain to make amends for all that I have done?*

What will Airel say when she reads that story? What will my father do when he returns? I feel his approach; it is imminent. Airel had so many questions, so much to learn, and so little time in which to live her life—which, really, if Ellie was honest about everything, should already have ended. *If not for Michael.*

She thought about leaving. Running. Trying to escape and hide, like she had done all those years before Qiel had been born.

Qiel.

She broke down and wept, falling to her knees on the kitchen floor, sobbing for her only son, moaning his name over and over again, pounding the stone with clenched fists. *Lost. Lost.*

I HAD TO TAKE a break from reading. My eyes were getting heavy, and trying to process all this information was giving me a headache.

The house was cold and the halls echoed as I walked, but I found my old room and threw myself down on my back on the big soft bed. It was strange, thinking of this place as home, but it felt more like home than my house did. So many things had happened here ... *things that changed me into what I am today.*

Crawling under the covers, I pulled them up to my chin and closed my eyes. I rolled my legs to one side, cracked my lower back, and grunted. I was still sore from our little rock-climbing adventure the other day.

There had only been six of us. Ellie, Dirk, Mark—Dirk's new best friend and a football jock—Nate, a rich kid who sneezed a lot, and Molly and Millie—twins who were really shy. All I knew about those two were their names. It often surprised me how many kids were at my school compared to how few I actually knew. I lived in my own world, and the last year or so didn't help matters.

I'd tried to get Michael to go with us. Our climbing guru, Shane, said it would be okay, but Michael bailed. I was more than a little annoyed, but I wasn't going to let it ruin a perfectly good day on the side of a cliff.

We took a small school bus and parked at Lucky Peak. Dirk sat next to Ellie across the aisle from me. I caught him staring at me a few times on the ride there and he didn't look away. The guy would not be shamed. But I was so excited to be climbing a real cliff that I didn't care.

Much.

"So, you scared of heights?" Dirk said.

I thought back to my last supersonic flight, the trail of blazing blue light that traced my path in the sky. I shook my head. "Nope."

Dirk seemed pleased. "But you could fall. I mean, rock climbing can be dangerous."

"Only if the guy on belay drops you."

Dirk blew a strand of dark hair from his face and shrugged. "You're heavy for a little girl. I caught you before you hit your head. No harm, no foul."

"Whatever."

We'd climbed at the YMCA five times, and Shane said I was best in class. But it wasn't really fair—I could fly, so it wasn't like I was scared of heights.

After we parked, we took our gear and hiked the short distance to the base of the cliffs. "We're here, everybody. Gear up," Shane said. "We climb in pairs. Stick with your partner and remember what you learned in the gym." Shane wore a fiber ball cap and a tight T-shirt. He was lean and fit. He climbed a few times a week, so his body was conditioned like crazy.

"Ready to tear it up?" Dirk asked me. I nodded.

Half an hour later, Dirk and I were sixty feet up the side of a crazy-high vertical cliff face. Even though he put on a brave façade, I could see he was nervous and getting more so the higher we climbed. I let him take the lead so he wouldn't see how easy it was for me. I was cheating a little, being superhuman, but it served him right for being a creeper.

"How you doing up there?" I asked. He was ten feet higher than I was, and a little to one side.

"Fine. How about you? You okay?"

"Yep. We're going a little slow, but if you're getting tired, I understand."

Dirk hammered in another anchor. "I have to hammer and set the anchors, and you get to climb and stare at my hot backside." He looked down at me, grinning.

I made a show of rolling my eyes. "You wish."

We were in a tough technical section where the rock face bulged outward. Based on what Shane had taught us, we could either go left or right, but Dirk was going up the middle. The last anchor he'd set was already fifteen feet below him. If he went a few feet more, he would be stuck. Either that, or he would have to jump six feet or so to get the next handhold. "I wish I'd made you lead."

I felt myself blush, but turned my face away. He would *not* see me blush. "You going left or right up there, buddy?"

Dirk was too far up. His right foot was on a round cone-shaped rock, but he should have had his left foot there. His left hung in midair while he searched for a place to put it, but there wasn't anything close by.

I could hear Shane giving some instructions from down below, but the main part of the group was far away from us. We were the better team, so we had taken the lead and gone first. Shane was on belay for the other team; we were basically free climbing.

"You okay, Dirk, or do you need a girl to help you?"

He didn't answer.

"Dirk?"

Silence.

He's seizing up. "I'm coming." I climbed as fast as I could without flying—I couldn't give myself away—and was about to reach him when he jumped for the next handhold. He didn't make it. For a split second, his hands had grip, but when his full weight came down, he slipped. The rope between us went slack and he fell.

If I didn't grab him quick, he would fall twenty feet and bounce off the cliff below me before the rope caught. I jumped, grabbing him around the waist. I helped him find his footing again, and as our eyes met, blood ran down from wounds in his left arm and forehead.

I jumped, sitting up in the bed. My nap had gone on long enough, and it was time to stop going over and over what had happened. There was nothing further I could do about it. *Dirk's okay—nobody saw what I did. It's all good.* I didn't believe it, though.

CHAPTER X

Arabia—788 B.C.

QIEL FELT COLD AND lonely. Something was happening to him that had never happened before. He was no fool; he knew enough from talking with friends about what would happen when boys began to become men. But this wasn't that. This was cold. He felt truly ill. His mind was filled with visions of horrifying monsters, tentacled beasts, things with scales and fins, the creature Leviathan.

His captor had shackled him here in this dark cell. A blacksmith had driven the pins through the manacles that chained him to the wall. He didn't know what had happened to his mother. He had wanted to cry earlier, but now he withheld all these fears, allowing them to coalesce inside of him, hardening into hatred, fury, even vengeance. He knew from what his mother had taught him that vengeance belonged to El alone, but still. He needed something to get through this. He would not allow himself to cry like a child. It was time to close the book on those chapters of his life. It was time to move forward into manhood now.

He pulled against the chains. They were heavy; he could barely pull them taut against their own sagging weight. A rat ran across his naked toes, its little claws raking across his skin, and he managed to get enough of a piece of it to kick it through the air, its hindquarters and its tail straight out as it spun. He growled and pulled on the chains harder, but they were too heavy. He shouted out in rage, feeling the man, but the voice that echoed back to him was that of a little boy who was frightened. Alone in the dark with the rats and chains.

He wanted more than anything to call out for his mother, to see if she was all right, but he withheld that, too. He didn't want to hear what such a cry might sound like if it echoed back to him in this place.

He dropped his hands to his sides and stood, puffing his hair out of his face as he breathed. Qiel felt cold. He retched onto the floor. Something was happening. Something his mother hadn't told him about.

A noise came to him then. It was the sound of dripping. His chains felt cold and moist, and his breath became visible as mist in the darkness. Yes. This was new. This was dangerous. He wasn't sure how he felt about it.

WHEN URIEL FINALLY CAME back to herself, she didn't know what had happened or how much time had gone by. She only knew the scalding shame of regret. She had been fool enough to think that Anael wouldn't be able to find her, and worse, that if he did, he would allow her to live out her life with Qiel in peace.

But no.

Her passion for destruction, her capacity for boundless hatred, had dissipated into dust over the last few centuries. It was scant enough as to have become immeasurable. "Anael," she called out in the darkness, rising to a sitting position. A sharp pain in her temples followed this sudden motion, and she held a hand to her head in response to it. She sobbed. "Anael." She hadn't known the feeling of desperation in centuries. "Anael!" she screamed at length, bringing on fresh pain and dizziness. She pressed both hands to her head and fell to her knees, doubled over.

Then, a voice. "Ready now?"

She didn't need to look up to know who it was. She sobbed again. Qiel had burned all the rebellion out of her heart. She hadn't thought such a thing could ever happen. All the senseless hatred had fled from her since her son had come into her life, and she knew what love was by having tasted it. "Your servant will do whatever you ask of her," she breathed. She could feel the wicked smile that spread itself on the hideous face of her foe in response.

"I will be Seer. You will bring me the Bloodstone, or your boy will never be free."

"Your servant wishes to see her son," she pleaded, breathing raggedly. She called out for him. "Qiel."

Laughter. "Preposterous. I cannot risk that, and you know it. Do not blame me for what you have wrought. I know your capabilities, Uriel. You shall not see him until the Bloodstone is in my hand. How else can I know that you will prove yourself trustworthy?" Anael then paused, and Uriel could hear him pacing back and forth.

"You dishonor me greatly, half-breed. You failed to fulfill the bargain we struck. I cannot say that I am surprised." He snorted.

Uriel felt a surge of anger. *How ironic that you also failed to supply the plans and strategy that would have fulfilled your side of it, scum.*

"As it happens," Anael said, "especially with you sons and daughters of dust, as your lives wear on, you *change.* Your young passions wither and rot. The motivations that once were pure and

undefiled—your many hatreds undiluted—wane as new seasons
break over you.

"But I know and see much," he spat at her. "I perceived that you
were delaying, that you were lying to me, that something profound
within you had changed and that you intended to dishonor both me
and the agreement. I knew that your heart had softened toward your
father even before I arranged for Yshmial's magnificent entrance
into your pitiful life. How poetic that a young man can seduce a
woman such as you. It is a delicacy rare indeed."

Uriel's eyes widened briefly and then clamped shut against a
swamping wave of grief.

"My task and aim are simple," Anael continued. "I require that
little red stone. You have both a weakness and a motivation, though
they are both specifically different now. Oh, yes, motivation for you
can still be found—a chink in your prodigious armor." He stood. "I
have found it. Now, bring me the Bloodstone, or your little boy will
rot in his chains and I will throw his lifeless husk to the birds so that
his bones may be picked clean. I will bring you to heel."

She sobbed once more, but then managed to control herself.
"Your servant will do as you command." She looked up at him, a
dark silhouette barely visible in the dank light of a solitary distant
torch. "I will bring you the stone."

She then vanished from view.

YAMANU SAT WITH ZEDKIEL by the fire late into the night,
trying to be quiet, to sense what he was missing.

Outside Zed's house, in the streets of Ke'elei, none moved but
a few scattered sentries on their rounds. Most of the guards were on
the wall or at the main gate as usual. Though appearances insisted

by peaceful witness that all was well, Yamanu felt unsettled.

"I wish Kreios were here," Zedkiel said.

Heaviness descended upon Yamanu. "As do I." He fell silent for a moment. "I am afraid Kreios has gone very far indeed, that he intends—it is clear now—not to return."

"I agree. I think further that he cannot. There is too much pain here."

Yamanu looked at Kreios's brother. "We all thought we knew what we were doing when we left paradise, did we not?"

Zed snorted, smoking his pipe, making ripples in the smoke that was pooling in his lap.

"And El allowed it." He sighed deeply. "El will not be surprised that we are learning a thing or two under the sun."

"We are learning about pain and loss."

Yam gestured to the bedrooms where Zedkiel's family used to sleep. "It was good while it lasted."

Zed nodded darkly. "She . . . they . . ." He gestured to both bedrooms, including his wife and his child, "died of old age hundreds of years ago now. But the pain remains."

"They lived good lives. Safe. And they now sleep, having been full of years under the sun. When El returns and paradise has come, when mankind has overcome, when they receive and share in the glory of El, the reunion will be sweet indeed."

Zedkiel looked at his angelic friend. "We thought we knew. But none of us knew how badly it would hurt to bury our families in the ground until that terrible unknown day. None of us could have imagined such a thing."

"Maria lived a full life, Zedkiel."

The other angel was silent. Evidently he had nothing to say.

"Do you feel it too?" Yamanu asked, changing the subject to what was really foremost upon the minds of both angels.

"Yes. Coming at us from under the earth," Zedkiel said.

"Yes."

Yamanu puffed on his pipe, considering things. *Whom can we tell?* Anael's counsel had grown dark indeed in centuries past, and the City of Refuge had become less and less resplendent, more and more like a festering scab upon the mountainside. There were hushed discussions amongst the Fallen, talk and rumor of some leaving Ke'elei for good, doing as Kreios had done. Perhaps there was a better life out there in the open.

Living cloistered like this seemed more and more reckless to Yamanu with each passing day, but it was not as if he could voice opinions like his to just anyone. Sentiments that were warm toward independence were frowned upon. Anael's council made free thinkers a spectacle, ostracizing them in the public hall and holding them up to open contempt and mockery.

Yamanu sighed. *It has come to this—the council lacks all sense. There can be no prophetic warnings anymore, no debates, no discussions. And even if we wish to flee, we must do it in secret. In the dead of night.* If Yamanu and Zedkiel—and whomever else happened to be a sympathizer—wanted to leave Ke'elei, they would be required to use the shadowing arts against their own kind and brethren. They would be forced to hide from El's own angels in order to take a chance at living by their convictions. *Has such a thing ever been done, even thought of?*

Yamanu reflected on these things. Increasingly now, he felt very strongly that the City of Refuge was not safe, and that they would be required to abandon it if they wished to make themselves so. *How odd,* he thought, *that Ke'elei should become a prison.* It was the exact opposite of the builders' intentions. That meant that there could only be one set of fingerprints on this latest development— they were all over it.

He shook his head and puffed on his pipe. His days were long and dark, and oh, how he craved for the light of day to dawn once more, and the feel of a sword in his hand.

CHAPTER XI

Elsewhere

THE KEEP OF THE Damned stood in Sheol high on a little snowy crag surrounded by incisor-like mountains on all sides. Bones were scattered in the yard and jutting through the snow. The house's thatched-roof gables were ornamented by upward-reaching carved gargoyles at their peaks, and the eaves drooped and were anchored to the ground on flying buttresses. A wide stair of stone descended from the great hall to the muddy ground. At the top of the stair, iron-banded double doors of black oak barred the entrance on the terrace. It appeared to be cruciform, a dark church or great hall of kings, its ornamentation and proportion both Scandinavian and Gothic. Pure white snow draped in billowed blankets over the thatch on the roof of the hall and on its stairs, jagged icicles hanging down here and there.

Kreios and Cain approached.

A lone figure, cloaked in red, stood above them upon the terrace, blocking the way into the hall. "Hail, murderer king. What, dost thou now come to the Keep of the Damned, Cain?"

"Ifrit," Cain said, standing tall.

The creature laughed at him.

"Master and ruler of the damned."

Instantly Ifrit disappeared—a wisp, a wraith—and reappeared before Cain at the bottom of the stair. It stooped to whisper into his ear. "Art thou here now at last, my keeper?" Ifrit snarled, and Kreios moved for his sword out of instinct.

Ifrit grabbed Kreios by the neck and pulled him off his feet. "And who are you to come here to the realm of the dead?" he said, wheeling Kreios around. The red cloak flickered and decomposed into ash as the demon cast off its humanoid husk and grew in size.

The demon was colossal, winged in black like the sails of a great ship. One of its arms was the size of Kreios.

Kreios pulled free of the demon's grip and then hovered over him with arms crossed. "There are many legends surrounding the mighty Ifrit. Are they mere folklore and myth, or are you the one whose name men speak in their nightmares?"

Ifrit roared and batted at Kreios, but he stayed just out of reach of the sharp claws that threatened to harm him.

"Who are you, Angel? How dare you speak of me as the one they call the Jinn. I am not a lowly genie. There is only one Ifrit. I was birthed under the sun from the blood of Abel, the first murder victim. The one who slayed that man now stands with you. Speak, or I will kill you quickly."

"Ifrit," Cain said, and then Ifrit turned away from Kreios. "Master of the Keep, this angel is the one called Death—Kreios, the Angel of El, Most High. He, not I, is your master."

The change was complete and immediate. Ifrit cowered, covering his face with his many wings, bowing low and trembling. "Say true? I did not know or I would not have laid my hands upon you. I beg for mercy, Kreios; I am yours." Ifrit again flickered, and like an old flame blown out, he changed form and reappeared as a man.

Kreios now spoke. "Ifrit, son of Abel, I know that you do not serve El or the evil one. You serve only death, and I am Death." Kreios came down and stood before the bowed demon. He was not angry, for he knew the master of the Keep was not permitted to go to the world above. He was a simple slave of his function, unless something were to change. When Ifrit took a soul in death, it passed to this place in solitude. Kreios knew of the Keep of the Damned because the Books spoke of it.

Cain had once been the master of the Keep, but El saw fit to make him finish his punishment under the sun. But these stories were the kind only told in the wind.

Ifrit stood before Kreios, his face now showing a flicker of hope. "Is the time now come?"

Kreios nodded. "I need you to take me into your Keep, to speak to the ones I have called to be kept in this place."

"I am the guard, the watcher of the gate and master of the Keep, but I have never entered there before, Kreios, Son of El. Only the first Master may bid us enter."

They both nodded toward Cain. "It is time," Kreios said.

"Lead us to your dead," Cain commanded.

These words were like a key in a lock and the great doors obeyed, the sound of the withdrawal of heavy iron locking bars ringing out like a dark bell tolling for the dead.

The three mounted the stairs with Ifrit in front, Cain behind and to his left, Kreios behind and to his right. The doors into the hall swung open as they set foot upon the terrace. They crossed the threshold into darkness.

The doors closed behind them, sealing them inside.

Ahead of them were a dais and a seat like a throne, a censer hanging by a cord from the ridge beam directly over it. Red-hot embers burned in the censer, and the smoke rose from it continually.

Whispers from the shadows came to their ears, and they said the same word again and again, redoubled upon itself a million times over. *"Cain."*

The three stood before the empty throne and looked up at the censer and the smoke that poured from it. In its weird light, Cain spoke. "You who murdered, hear now Death and obey." The sound of his voice produced ripples in the great hall, and the three could feel the dead startle and dart like great schools of fish all around them in the darkness.

More echoes of whispers sounded. *"Cain."*

Kreios spoke. "I have need of you once more. My voice called you to this place and now I call you from it. Rise to created life under the sun once more, and by fulfilling those works I will set forth, you will reap your reward."

The whispers changed. They now resounded millions upon millions of times. *"Ifrit."*

Ifrit spoke in response, confirming the command. "Let us rise."

The smoke pouring from the censer increased, thickening and blackening, like ink in water. Finally the censer burst and fell, the embers it once contained raining fire down upon the dais and the throne, consuming it. The great doors through which the three had entered were now thrown open outward and tossed aside, their iron hinge pins bent and cracked.

The Keep was broken, and the dead poured out of it. Kreios flew out of the grave at their head, and the gathering darkness surrounded him. He was Death. Now all of his own were at his command.

CHAPTER XII

Arabia—788 B.C.

URIEL HEADED TO DUMAH, the resting place of the cursed Bloodstone.

She knew where the stone was, had always known because in her youth she took it from the counterfeit Seer's neck and killed him in his sleep. She'd hidden it, hoping that without the power it held, the world would leave her alone.

She hated that she had to bow to her new master most foul, Anael, the vilest traitor she had ever known. Mostly, though, she feared the Bloodstone and what it might do to her. For, though she did indeed have reason to leave her pact with Anael unfulfilled all these years because of her softening heart, most of her reluctance was bound up in a palpable fear of what effect the Bloodstone might exert upon her.

Dumah was in the middle of the great Arabian Desert. She hovered in and around the place, sensing her environs and shadowing her presence from her enemies, seeking out the Bloodstone. They were close, camped in the valley close to Mard Castle. It would be days, if not hours, before they found her hiding place. Time was running out, and now her son's life too was on the line.

She could feel it calling to her. She began to move toward it.

Alarming thoughts began to resound within her soul. She thought of how the Prince of Darkness would desire an allegiance with one like her, how the power of his strategies would be amplified through her if she were to allow herself to become overwhelmed by the drug of the Bloodstone. She had heard many things about the Bloodstone and its associations with Lucifer, but now all rumors were cast aside and she knew—the stone embodied the Day Star himself. It was undeniable.

She flowed like fragrance through the cracks in Mard Castle's stone walls, her essence being drawn onward through chinks and breaks, upward into the highest of the four towers of the citadel. There, in a hidden part in the east wall, the Bloodstone pulsed and seethed with hatred, calling her onward to her destiny. Uriel did not manifest in the flesh, but used her essence to surround the object for transport.

That was when her plans failed, for as she embraced the stone, it sucked her down and into itself. She became a part of it then. Such an event she did not foresee. She did not have time to repent of her foolishness. She was overwhelmed with cold darkness. Her end was at hand. She was face-to-face with her worst fears.

QIEL THOUGHT OF HIS mother, and of the man who took him and chained him in the dark. Pulling again, he raged, twisting his body one way and then the other, but the heavy chains held him fast.

Something was happening to him. He vomited on the floor and realized that he was standing in water. It covered his feet, it dripped

from the walls, and as if on his command, the water moved in, out
… with the thudding of his heart.

A sound beyond the walls of stone thundered like the sea.

No. No, it is the sea.

"Mother." It was a cry, a plea, and a prayer. He was afraid, so he
closed his eyes and tried to act like a man. Qiel wasn't sure why, but
he knew these stones that had held him in his cell were not going to
hold him much longer.

He pulled on the heavy chains with both arms at the same time.
His back arched, the water rose, and with each pull, the ground
under his feet bulged and relaxed, bulged and relaxed.

Were the stories true? Had the powers of the old ones vanished,
as some believed? *Or is it possible some still exist?* Questions filled
his mind, and then the memory of his mother falling in front of him
by the hand of the man with the blowgun—dead, for all he knew—
brought his attention back to the very face of all his fears.

Qiel knew he should be terrified, scared out of his mind to see
water like fingers twisting through the cracks in the walls, raining
down from the domed ceiling. But now he laughed, for it was
becoming clear to him that the water was not here to harm him. He
was the one bringing it here, and it was his to move however he
wished.

With the final pull, the once-heavy chains came apart, snapping
from his wrists as if made of dry parchment. The ground boiled
under him, white water rushing in, lifting him up as the room filled.

Then, real dread grabbed hold of him. *I do not know how to
swim. I really am going to drown.*

Thin rays of light pierced his dark cell from above, and as he
struggled against the ceiling, he took one last breath and then sank
under. He began to panic.

I am sorry, Mother. I have failed both of us.

More light filled the room as the far wall began to crumble under the weight of the water. Qiel watched this and began to hope again. The wall could fall, and he could be set free, *but will it happen in enough time?* The breath he had drawn was now stale, and his lungs burned with the effort it took to hold it. He burst and let it go, breathing in a lungful of water.

To his great surprise, it didn't hurt like he thought it would. He could breathe it. It was different, but breathing out and in a few times, he realized he was still alive—he would be fine.

The stones of the wall began to move farther apart and then fell away. He could see, as the waters poured out, that he was high up above the ground; his cell hadn't been subterranean, as he had supposed. He had been imprisoned in a tower.

Far below, in the oppressive light of the Arabian Desert sun, he could see one of the guards gaping in astonishment from the pile of rubble below and then upward to him as he stood on the edge of the ruined tower. Water poured from his broken cell and he coughed up what remained of it in his lungs. Twisting tentacles of water hung in the air at his sides, and as he lifted one arm, the tentacle reacted to his movement.

Qiel now felt this new power surging through him, and he heard the crashing of many powerful waves resounding in his head. As they broke over his mind, he and the water launched out of the tower into the air and down to the earth, crashing and breaking over the sands in a tide of irresistible power. The rush of the waters delivered Qiel into the wide open, crushing the lone guard under its weight. The waters then receded, absorbed into the dry sands that greedily received them.

He realized then that he had changed completely. He had become what his mother long feared he would become—one of the Sons of El.

Soaked, Qiel slowly stood to his feet and looked around him, blinking his eyes.

I'm free.

He turned and ran.

CHAPTER XIII

Sawtooth Mountains of Idaho—Present Day

MY READING OF THE Book of Kreios was interrupted by the arrival of the very angel who bore that name. It wasn't as if trumpets sounded or the world ended or anything. He walked into the library and sat down opposite me, near the fire, and regarded me.

I peeked at him over the top of his Book. "Oh. Hi." I swallowed hard, feeling a bit like a kid caught doing something she knew was wrong. I wanted to run to him and hug him, but I didn't. By the time I had thought it through, the opportunity had passed. Something didn't feel right about it.

As he sat there, his fingertips made a tent before him, and he studied me. "I am glad you are well, Airel." There was considerable weight in this statement, as if there were more to it than just little old me and my well-being. He nodded toward the Book as I closed it and placed it on my lap. "Has my Book shown you something new?"

"Yes, I was reading up on—"

"Please." He raised a hand in objection. "Do not tell me."

"Why not?" I was flustered.

He sighed, heavy. "Because there are things in my Book that I do not desire to be made plain. Ignorance is sometimes requisite for a sound mind to continue to remain sound."

"What do you mean, don't tell you—why not?" My tone was a little disrespectful, and I didn't mean for my words to pop out of my mouth like that.

The expression on his face immediately made me regret it. "I do not want to know about everything that is to come. What my Book reveals to you is for you, and is not for me. Keep close to your heart what it shows you, Airel, and do not tell a soul what you have seen and been allowed to imagine there. Some of us may not be as strong as you are."

What does that mean?

Just then, Ellie walked into the library, her eyes puffy and red like she'd been crying. Crying hard. "Hello, Dad."

Kreios stood. "Daughter. Are you well?"

She took a halting breath and glanced my way for a split second. "As well as I should be, I suppose. And you?"

Kreios grunted, obviously ill at ease. "The same."

I sat looking back and forth between them for what felt like an eternity, the tension of awkwardness in the room growing by the second. There was obviously something each of them was carrying, something they had chosen to keep to themselves, something they desperately needed help with—and further, something they each stubbornly tried to carry on with, going solo. "Can I get anyone anything?" I asked as I stood, the Book of Kreios in my hands.

"Not hungry," they said in unison without acknowledging me.

That feeling of a storm about to break washed over me and I shifted my feet, not sure what to do or say.

"Maybe you should go, Airel," Ellie said, her eyes now glued to the floor.

I shook my head in a reflexive twitch of disbelief. "Uh…okay, I guess." I started walking away, and my annoyance got the better of me. "Hey, maybe you guys should go down to the dojo to talk. You know, so you don't like, break anything up here that's . . ." I cleared my throat. "Rare and … and, you know, irreplaceable." I swallowed; I needed air badly. "Uh, should I take your car, then?" I asked her.

"Keys are in it," she said. "I'll see you back in town."

"Later tonight?"

"You know that's kinda irrelevant up here," she said.

I growled. She was right. And I hated that. "Fine." I put the Book down on the table and walked out of the library. I went down the torch-lit hallway toward the staircase that ascended into the clearing with the old door lying in the dirt, turned the knob, and reentered the real world. My mind wanted to place those words in quotes inside my head because I wasn't so sure how real it actually was to me anymore.

I turned the key in Ellie's Toyota FJ and the engine came to life. It could get me back into town in about five hours.

As I drove down the lumpy dirt road toward the highway, I thought, *El, why is life so freaking hard?* I made a fist and banged on the steering wheel and said, "Drama. Yay." Yeah, I totally needed more of that.

ELLIE WAS THE FIRST to be seated. "So, Father, how have you really been?"

Kreios remained standing in his library. "I assume El instructed you to show her my Book once again?"

"Yes, Father. I wouldn't have done it if otherwise."

He grunted. "Because you know the risks in regard to free will." He placed his Book back up where it belonged, on the mantel above the fireplace.

Ellie resisted the urge to roll her eyes at him. "Yes, of course. Will you please sit down with me and talk?"

Kreios considered this for a moment, and then sat across from her.

Ellie leaned forward. "I wanted to thank you for what you did in South Africa."

Kreios looked at her. "You are welcome." He appeared to think about his next words. "It was …what else could I have done?"

Ellie agreed with a wag of her head. "Well, thank you anyway. I wouldn't be here if you hadn't …"

"Speak no more of it, Ur—Ellie."

"I'm really sorry…"

"Please, daughter." Pain showed plainly on his face. "There is no need. All has been forgiven."

"But Father," she said, her voice desperate, "after Ke'elei … after Qiel … after everything I have done, there must be some need I can fill, something I can do, some way I can show how much I regret—"

"Ellie …" Kreios closed his eyes. "It is enough, what you've been doing for Airel."

"But still," she said softly. "I thought if I could protect Airel, if I could instruct her, keep her from being overtaken by the Brotherhood, I could undo the damage I caused and …"

Kreios stood and came to her and cradled her face in his hands. "Daughter. Ellie. Uriel. Look at me."

She did, reluctantly.

"I love you. And that is all that matters."

She fell into his arms and wept. She felt like a child again, held by her father. She closed her eyes, wishing this moment would never end.

CHAPTER XIV

Boise, Idaho—Present Day

FOR WHATEVER REASON, WHEN I got back into the city limits of Boise, I didn't feel like going home. Mom wasn't expecting me for another day or two and I was unsettled.

Was it dishonest, what I was thinking of doing? Technically, yeah. *"Which means yes,"* She interjected, prompting a vicious roll of the eyes from yours truly.

"Nice of you to show up," I shot back, but *She* didn't respond. *Figures,* I thought.

I spent a little while driving aimlessly around the city. I turned up Reserve into the foothills toward Table Rock, but it was after dark and the gate that led up to the mesa was closed and it was cold out, so I turned around and let the headlights drift me back down toward Boise.

I wasn't sure how or why exactly, but eventually I ended up parked alongside the curb on the street near Michael's foster parents' house. I wasn't sure what I was doing. It was late, way past my curfew, and I couldn't have reasonably expected to be able to see him. What was I going to do? Throw pebbles at his bedroom window? Wake him up with "But soft, what light through yonder window breaks" in a mind-contorting Shakespearean role reversal?

I felt pathetic, sitting there behind the wheel of that car. I couldn't get my mind off myself and how my life had slipped so far out of my grasp, how my plans for my future had missed the mark by such an appalling measure. That's when *She* piped up again.

"It's not about you. Get ready, Airel. The time is coming soon when you will have to prove what you believe with action, with deed. Go beyond the words. Get ready."

I was trying to take in this new information and decipher the meaning when I saw a shadow in the rearview mirror. My eyes darted toward it, and my heart started racing. Then, right outside the driver's side door, I felt a presence. Before I could turn and look, there was a *tap tap* on the glass and I tried to inhale all the air inside the car, gasping in fright.

I turned to see Michael standing there, a playful smirk spreading over his face as the realization that he had scared the daylights out of me dawned on him. "Michael. What the—" I opened the door a little harder than necessary, banging in into his knees.

"Ow," he said.

"Oh, did I do that?" I got out and stood in the dark predawn street with my boyfriend. "So sorry," I teased. I wasn't sure what kind of mood he would be in, so I waited to see how he would respond.

"Airel, what are you doing here?" His voice was low, flat.

Quick. Come up with something. "Me? What are *you* doing, prowling the streets like a criminal?" It sounded good in my head.

"Really, Airel? I live here now, remember?" He shoved his hands in his pockets and looked over his shoulder toward his new house, where his now so-called family slept. "I don't know what to say anymore, Airel. You didn't text me all day—you never do anymore."

I shrugged. "I was with Ellie. Kreios is back, if you care to know."

"Yeah, I care to know. Why would you say that?" His eyes were dark and I shivered.

I looked around. Fog was rolling in, as was common at this time of year in the wee hours, and the streetlamp in the distance was bathing this river of mist in a chemist's pallid yellow. "Come on, get in. At least we can talk without freezing to death." I jerked my head, motioning to the passenger side of the FJ.

He walked around, and we both jumped in. As the doors closed, he met me in the middle of the car, both hands around my face, pulling me toward him, kissing me full on the lips passionately. I was so shocked at his forwardness that I wasn't sure what to do. I kissed him back for a second or two, and enjoyed it, but as his hands fell to my shoulders and pulled me in tighter, I began to feel unsafe.

"Michael," I mumbled into his face. I pushed against him, but he wasn't catching the hint. "Michael," I mumbled again, but it got me nowhere. His hands started moving around from my arms to my chest, so I bit him. Hard.

"Ow." He withdrew, touching his lip.

"Michael. Get control of yourself," I said, feeling alarmed. "What are you doing? We were talking and you—I mean, what is wrong with you?"

He was angry with me. "First you stalk me in the middle of the night, and then when I try to give you what I think you're after, you freaking *bite* me. Aw. There's blood. What's wrong with *me*— what's wrong with you?"

"Me?" I could see that there was something different about him. A little less man, a little more boy, and a bunch of excuses for a crutch. I used to love the way he would change from hard-muscled man to cute, innocent boy with only a smile, but now I wondered what I was missing. The man I loved, the boy I had fallen for was not sitting across from me right now. He repelled me a little.

"Michael," I said, "what's happened to you lately?"

He turned away. "I don't know. Things are not good." His voice was inarticulate—it was dead monotone. "Not like I need a perfect life, but I can't shake this …" He trailed off and wouldn't turn my way.

It was true then. What I had been feeling about him—and yet had been unable to materialize even in my feelings—was true; my intuition was correct. He was changing, and not for the better. I wondered if maybe he wasn't dealing with the loss of his dad so well, if maybe his foster family wasn't providing him with all he needed right now.

Or maybe it was something else entirely.

"What do you mean, 'not good'?" I said. "Are you okay at home? Did they do something to you?" The hair on my arms stood up, and I could feel *She* come to full attention in the back of my mind. The words *"Get ready"* kept echoing inside me, and I felt like I was about to face down some demonic behemoth once more. *But this is Michael…*

Still staring out the window into the cold darkness, he shook his head. "No, nothing like that." Now his eyes caught mine, and they were like knives. "When I say, 'not good', I mean with you. I feel like you're a million miles away. We've been through so much, and now you're just … I don't know. This is stupid."

As I touched his arm, I tried to hold back the tears that wanted to overflow. "Michael, I love you with all my heart. I know it's been hard and things are a mess, but it'll get better. We'll get through this—together."

His eyes narrowed, the rags of hate and pain so clear in the windows to his soul that it hurt me and I had to turn away. "Airel, you don't have a clue, do you?" His voice was low and threatening.

I shivered again and my gut balled up into what felt like a stone. "What are you even talking about? What did *I* do, Michael? Can you tell me that? I mean," I paused and swallowed hard. "Do you love me anymore? Do you still feel anything for me?" My voice cracked. Then the question I'd hoped I would never have to ask slipped from my mouth. "Did you ever?"

He laughed, using the back of his hand to wipe blood from his lower lip. I was struck sick by how much like Stanley Alexander he looked in that moment. "You asking me a thing like that is one of the reasons. After all we have seen, after my father—"

"Michael … I'm really confused right now, babe." Tears spilled down my cheeks. I wanted so badly to skip backward, start this conversation all over and give more of myself to him so he understood how I felt. I needed him to feel me, to break past whatever wall he'd built so I could get inside to where *my* Michael was.

His eyes were moist around the edges, and his voice was thick with emotion. "Airel, it's probably best that you don't come around anymore."

I could have spoken the words before he said them. I knew what he was going to say, but it still didn't shock me any less to hear him say it. I was speechless.

He opened his door. "I'm going to do the honorable thing now and leave." He stood, turned back toward me, and leaned in. "That's what you wanted, right?" I watched as his face contorted from simple pain into animal rage. He drew back, opened the door as wide as possible, and then slammed it so hard I thought the glass would shatter. He stared at me through the window, breathing hard and pointing down the road in front of me. I saw it in his eyes. It was as if I'd ripped his heart out and then spit in his face, and after all we'd been through together. I wanted to go to him, make him understand somehow, but how could I when *I* didn't even understand what had just happened?

I started the car and left.

Michael Alexander had broken up with me.

CHAPTER XV

I HAD DRIVEN ALL the way out to Ontario, right on the other side of the Idaho-Oregon border, by the time I came to my senses. I turned around on the first overpass, crossed back over the Snake River, and pulled the FJ into the Idaho welcome center rest area. I got out and walked to the bluff that overlooked the river, the empty snow-covered corn fields stretching out in late autumnal slumber just beyond.

Time didn't register. I couldn't even remember how I'd ended up over here or where I'd driven all night. I was only a half an hour from Boise, but somewhere in the night I lost track; all I could hear was Michael telling me to leave. I was numb and wordless as my mind replayed our conversation over and over again.

If there was any hard and fast rule for my life, it was that there was no hard and fast rule, no common thread that could provide meaning or context. *Is this what womanhood is? Is this what I have to look forward to for the rest of my life?*

I stood in the cold feeling like a ghost, watching my breath rise and cool to be carried away by the harsh dead winds that whipped at me. I stared at the river below as the sun rose behind me. When the first orange-red rays shot forth from the sun to cast the opening shadows of the day, I had made my decision—I needed sanctuary.

That was what I wanted more than anything. I wanted to go to a place that was safe for me, to be alone and think all these things over, try to get my arms around what was happening in my life, try to make sense of it all.

So it would be the public library, then.

But first, I needed breakfast. I was starving. And I wanted my coconut latté fix too, so I drove back into town intending to stop in at Moxie for a while, to take some time to breathe. But then I realized that I had too many memories there. I certainly couldn't go to my regular coffee shop, the one where I had first met Michael. Not right now. *Perhaps never again.* I realized that someone or something had been working very hard to take even this away from me. It pissed me off beyond words.

This new crisis produced a mild conundrum as to whether or not I would suffer myself to brave the domain of the green mermaid and burnt gunko. *Maybe I should try something else entirely.*

I ended up grabbing a table at Denny's, for crying out loud.

It was the only place I could think of that might allow me to go both unnoticed and unmolested. In other words, it wasn't Moxie, it wasn't the Sunrise Café—it wasn't any number of places I had ever been with Kim or Michael or Ellie or James the demon boy or anyone else.

I was so frustrated—everything had been taken from me. I kept my head down all through my meal, scrolling through my social media "news" feeds on my phone. Big surprise—there was nothing happening in my world. But of course, everyone had their little OMG moments in their status updates, freaking out about meaningless nonsense. The usual.

After breakfast, I sought refuge in my sanctuary—the public library by my house. That was my go-to place whenever I felt harried or overwhelmed. It was calming for me.

I felt a deep need for poetry. I could taste my own hunger for it.

I knew where I was going. The Dewey Decimal System wasn't as relevant to me as the physical layout of the place was—I knew which shelf I wanted. And though I was no expert, I at least knew a little Frost, a little Whitman. I knew they might have something to cure what ailed me.

As I approached the correct part of the stacks, I noticed a guy about my age in the poetry section. He was lying propped up on the carpet on his elbows, a notebook and his phone nearby, a volume in his hand, totally engrossed. As I got closer, I recognized him. Black hair, cool jeans, distressed T-shirt with a soda-pop logo on it. Dirk Elliot.

As I got closer, he looked up, flashing me a little embarrassed smile.

I didn't know what to think, so I said, "Camping out in the poetry section?"

He smiled and laughed. "Yeah, I found this book and got sucked in. I got here early. Sorry if it looks like I think I own the place."

"Hey, don't mind me," I said. "What are you reading?"

"Tennyson."

I knew the name, but not the work. Not really. "Must be good."

He looked at me as if he were tasting something he loved. "It is."

"I'm partial to Blake lately, myself."

I took a volume from the shelf and walked to a table in the back corner of the library, away from Dirk, away from everyone. Feeling as if I had escaped something, I began to read.

Glasgow, Scotland—Present Day

A FEW FLOORS ABOVE the rainy streets of Glasgow, Jordan

Weston sat behind his desk as Valac presented the spoils to him. "The Bloodstone, my lord, and a gift I thought you might enjoy." Valac did not bow before the half-dead man as he was merely a paying client, nothing more.

"You have done well thus far," Jordan Weston said to Valac, his procurement contractor. "And the girl Airel?"

"Soon."

Jordan took the heavy Book with his un-good hand, placing it on the desk. It *was* her Book, the Book of Airel. He did not dare touch it with his other hand. "The only missing piece now is for the true heir to be found." He would not let the boy Michael take what was not his.

"I hear she's dangerous … able even to destroy the Brotherhood if she so chooses," Valac said.

Jordan thought about it. *If we cannot find the Other, we may need the girl—the half-breed Airel.* She had more power in some respects than her grandfather Kreios did, at least judging by reports of what had happened in Cape Town. "She is powerful, yes. But she has yet to realize her true ability."

"Allowing her to live is a big gamble on your part."

"I suppose so," Jordan said. He searched Valac's eyes and said, "You reckon it's best to kill her, then."

Valac shrugged and changed the subject. "I will have to call you 'Seer' the next time we meet. That Stone is sought by the Brothers as well as the Sons of El. I should have charged more for its return; it took some doing." Valac was wearing a black fitted suit and a blood-red tie; he had a flair for the understated irony of such things.

"And yet clearly you enjoyed your work, so what's to complain about?" Jordan began writing out a company check—Valac's wages. "The Seer is not a position to be taken," Jordan said. "It is a birthright. I am not of the bloodline and I do not assume that I would be worthy even if I were. Not all seek total power." He watched Valac's reactions carefully. He didn't want to play the wrong cards in this game; Valac was ruthless.

"I see." Valac took the check Jordan offered, stuffing it into his breast pocket. "So you're doing this because you're bored, because you lack spice in your life? You could find yourself a nice dead girl to settle down with—"

Jordan showed him his fangs. Valac took a step back, a smile crossing his face, holding up both hands in mock surrender. "Sorry to offend—lord."

The little shape shifter is lucky I'm a master of self-control. "I will pay you twice what you have there if you can bring me the half-breed Airel. Alive. I prefer my corpses to be warm, and I will relish killing her."

"Very well. I shall bring her to you."

"Then be gone."

Valac snorted and left with a wicked smirk on his face.

It was raining again, and that meant pain in the un-good hand. Jordan held the Bloodstone in that one; he made sure to only ever touch it with that one. Even so, he could feel its power, the call and the need. He was no fool—the Bloodstone took one's *soul.* He didn't want to find out what would happen to him—he didn't have one of those.

Boise, Idaho—Present Day

I LOOKED UP FROM the table to see that Dirk had decided to join me. I smiled politely at him as he sat down across from me. He took that as an invitation to chat me up, which I resented. I had come here for solace, not to get hit on.

"So, how are you and Michael doing?"

I tried not to let my kneejerk reaction, which tended toward panic, betray the truth. I cleared my throat and improvised, "Oh, you know. My parents have had me on this early curfew thing lately. So we don't get to see much of each other."

"That good, huh? Sorry, I should have kept my big trap shut."

Now I felt bad. Without even thinking about it, I reached across and touched his hand. There was a little zap of static electricity. "Ow, sorry," I whispered. "I hate when that happens."

He rubbed his hand against his shirt and chuckled. "It's okay. I think the books have their own kind of electricity. Either that, or we seem to have a spark or something."

I sat there wondering if Dirk had been waiting for Michael and me to break up so he could make his move. "About Michael, though, it's okay. I mean, how could you know?" I said that with the slightest amount of malicious intent.

He smirked. "Exactly. I was only trying to be friendly. I know things have been tough for you this past year. Word gets around. Thought you could use a friend, that's all." He tapped his finger on the table and looked up at me.

Why does he have to be here now, and why can't he be some fugly guy? "It's okay," I managed to say, not feeling my normal self at all. Michael wasn't himself either; I didn't feel like I even knew him anymore. *How about this Dirk character?* Here was a guy sitting right across from me who *wanted* to be with me. *If I like that idea, is it so wrong?*

"Hey," he said, a look of concern mixed with something else passing like a shadow across his face, "are you okay?"

I felt like crying again, like being held, like being comforted. I could never deny my love for Michael, that I would always love him. *But why do I have to be the only one to hold on, and why is it so hard? And why is it that all I can think about right now is what it might be like to be with Dirk?*

"YOU DON'T LOOK SO well," Valac said, ecstatic at how perfectly it had all played out. She reached out and touched me so quickly; I barely had to work on her at all.

"I … I feel lightheaded," Airel said.

Valac knew precisely why. That hadn't been mere static electricity; it had been a spiritual discharge. Energy had changed hands and crossed between them, from Airel to him, in that touch. *The sons of dust know so very little about the power of touch,* he mused, *even though the evidence is right before their eyes, even in their holiest of their books.* He was thankful that almost none of them took these things literally, or even seriously, anymore. "We should get you to the bathroom, maybe splash some water on your face. You look like you need some air."

Valac, still appearing to be Dirk, came around to Airel's side of the table and grasped her by the arms, helping her to her feet. *This is where it will happen. It will be now.* As he held the half-breed by her arms, another, larger exchange occurred, and he began to drain the power and life out of Airel through his hands in larger amounts.

They wouldn't make it anywhere near the bathrooms. As Airel turned to walk that way, Valac pulled her close. She looked up at him, seeing only Dirk, and tried to say something. He leaned down and kissed her, softly at first, more life draining from her into him. He could feel her pull back at first, but then she leaned into him, animal desire taking her over.

She kissed him harder, her hands gripping his back and pulling him closer. "Dirk," she mumbled stupidly.

Lambs to the slaughter. Valac knew his training well, and he had read the brief on this one. Airel was different—able to wield the Sword of Light, descendant of Kreios, El's Angel of Death, supposedly immune to the drain of the Brotherhood—at least with that Sword. Various theories had been posited within the intelligence circles of his clan. One of the more plausible had been that this angel spawn could be drained, maybe even killed, if only an insurgent could get close enough to lay hands on her. *Hypothesis verified,* Valac thought, smiling. *And only I could have done it.*

Airel collapsed into his arms, and Valac lowered her to the floor. He looked around. They hadn't taken two steps away from the table she had picked out in the back. It was still pretty early too, and on a weekday morning, so there weren't many people around. He shoved her wide-eyed but lifeless husk under the table like a sack of potatoes, and then really got to work.

He cradled Airel's head in both hands and began feeding in earnest upon the power of her life force, feeling her fears and trepidations, licking up the burning fumes of her attempts and failures and closing them away inside his greedy heart, his dead soul.

I am going to drain you dry.

ABOUT THE AUTHORS

Aaron Patterson

AARON IS THE USA TODAY Bestselling author of over 10
novels. He was homeschooled and grew up in the west. Aaron loved
to read as a small child and would often be found behind a book,
reading one to three a day on average. This love drove him to want
to write, but he never thought he had the talent. He wrote Sweet
Dreams, his first book, in 2008. He lives in Boise, Idaho, with his
family, Soleil, Kale, and Klayton. His daughter had an imaginary
friend named She.

Chris White

YOU KNOW WHAT THEY say—that behind every great man is
an unstoppable rebel force—and it's true. Like Moriarty was to
Holmes, C.P. White is the reversed polarity doppelganger behind
it all. He blogs about weirdness on the C.P. White Media Blog and
spins dark tales, psychological thrillers that you'll want to read
with the lights on. He works in the front office writing romantic
YA paranormal fiction with Aaron Patterson, collaborates with
illustrator Joey Zavaleta on the Great Jammy Adventure children's
books, and even plays sometime editor to his award-winning author
friends. Both personalities will fight to the death for a bowl of high
quality mac-n-cheese. C.P. doesn't mind living with spiders, but
only because his house is old and they were there first. He prefers
riding bikes and playing nice, he dislikes boring people on general
principle, and is apt to launch bottle rockets through open windows.
Both agree that their least favorite thing is dog exhaust on the
bottom of their shoe. You can learn more about author Chris White,
as well as author C.P. White, at http://www.cpwhitemedia.com.

Look for the *Last* book in the Airel Saga:

URIEL

THE PRICE

Book 6, Part 11-12